Fresh from her magical holiday at the fossmere and her first screen test in over a decade, Pippin Pearmain travels from Sydney to Delphinium Island to attend a dance festival and to appear in an indie film. From her arrival at the festival it's all go, dancing to new tunes, meeting the other performers, and taking a chance to have her ballet, *Delphine*, workshopped with a real dance troupe. Filming the first scenes of *Half-Life of the Lost* is another challenge, as Pip has to perform unscripted.

While indulging in a bit of peace in a supposedly empty barn, Pip unexpectedly encounters someone she knew many years ago. Their connection dates from their shared love of the book Grandmother's Sunshine, the mysterious family treasure that even the knowledgeable Jonquil from *The Orange Grove* bookshop believes does not exist. Pip has a new dilemma. Is a treasure shared a treasure diminished?

Performing Pippin Pearmain 5
Copyright © 2023 Lark Westerly
ISBN: 978-1-4874-3717-6
Cover art by Martine Jardin

Published by eXtasy Books Inc

Look for us online at:
www.eXtasybooks.com

PERFORMING PIPPIN PEARMAIN 5

BY

LARK WESTERLY

DEDICATION

For those who take up new occupations when they're already over-committed.

Author's Note

Fiction and Reality

Major places in this story, such as Tasmania, the city of Sydney and the state of Victoria certainly do exist. So does Bass Strait. The towns of Jellico Bay and Delmsford are made up, as is Delphinium Island. The suburb of Windhill with its Fairy Gardens is made up. If it existed, it would be somewhere near North Sydney. Gilchrist would be near Cremorne. The suburb of Glebe is real as is the iconic Sydney Harbour Bridge. Magda's preferred tipple, Tom Cat Hill single malt, is made up. The ship *Lenten Rose,* which sank the year Rose and Hellebore Laurel were born, is also invented. Merimbula, where Edgar Treadwell was born, is a real place, 500 km south of Sydney. The instrument Costas Capricorn plays, the amphora horn, does not exist, but Mim's spinet is one of the forerunners of the modern piano.

Pip's story covers a year, taking her from her reclusive cottage in Jellico Bay to her old hometown of Delmsford, to the magical fossmere, on to Sydney and thence to Delphinium Island. The nine books compile into one continuing story, slowly revealing the mystery and magic that has been part of Pip's world all along.

And how did I come to write Pip's story? It all began in February 2022 with a flower show . . . and with a bucket.

The story so far . . .
Book One
Introducing   Pippin   Pearmain—small,   eccentric,

determined, sixty-six, and ruled by cats. Until a decade ago, Pip earned her living by playing offbeat roles on stage and screen, but after her mother and her agent died in the same week, parts dried up and she moved to Jellico Bay. During a visit to her old hometown she encountered her cousins, Lupin de Leon and Juniper *Jan* Sharman. They, and Jan's daughter, Clarkia, were the only remaining members of the Laurel-Pearmain-de-Leon family. Over afternoon tea at the Delmsford Flower Show, Pip revealed her long-held secret — her bucket list — a literal list of interesting buckets. In return, her cousins wrote down their secrets.

Home in her cottage with the original cat and the back-up cat, who communicate with her in what she thinks of as Cat-Morse, Pip read the secrets. Jan revealed herself as the novelist Juniper Gin. Lupin's secret was shocking — she had just a few months to live.

After Lupin's passing, Jan met the cats, Kittisack and Amberjill, and received a bucket Pip had promised her for Lupin's last repose. They discussed the provenance of a family heirloom — two copies of a book called *Grandmother's Sunshine*. Lacking heirs, Pip had once offered her copy to a young friend, whose mother refused to let her accept it. A call from Jan's daughter prompted Jan to dash off, leaving Pip with Lupin's legacy — an envelope and a pottery cat.

Book Two

Pip received a call from Magda Saxer, announcing herself as Pip's new agent and offering a role in a film called *Half-Life of the Lost*. The cats were unexpectedly in favour. They suggested Jan's daughter would come to look after them.

Lupin's envelope contained a voucher written in disappearing ink. Pip called the information line, whereupon Gerry Trip, Lupin's ex-colleague at Vouch-Safe, informed her she had one hour to prepare for a mystery Experience.

Gerry's step-grandson, Jamie, promised to cat-sit. He drove Pip to a rendezvous.

Pip boarded the yacht *Tulpenmanie*, crewed by pleasant Zach, his odd girlfriend, Jisinia, and Jamie's uncle, Tane.

When Pip realised Tane was missing, she called triple zero. Jisinia confiscated the phone but returned it. Pip rationalised that Tane must have returned to shore.

That night, Tane, who was a silversmith, came back. After resizing a ring for her, he invited Pip to meet his family. She agreed.

Tane picked her up and jumped into the sea.

Book Three
Tane took Pip through an underwater gateway to *over there* where she spent a week with his extended family, practising ballet with Jane and making friends with Tane's spouse, Jillian Jules. The fossmere, a waterfall pool, delighted Pip. She left her tektite ring in the cave behind the falls in gratitude for her adventure. Tane and Jules took her to Hob's Island where she added a new bucket to her list. A sighting of dolphins gave her the idea for a ballet.

Back at Lemonwood Cottage, Pip discovered Jamie, her driver, was a *mutie* or *mutable fay*. He had a second self — a dog he called Kakao.

Jan asked if her daughter Clarkia might come to stay at Lemonwood Cottage while Pip had her screen test.

Book Four
Pip met her agent, Magda, at Sydney airport. Magda's friend, Pandora, drove them to a guesthouse run by Edgar and Joan Treadwell. Next morning, Edgar took Pip to a grassy area *over there* to do her ballet practice.

Pip went with Magda to *Diamond Spellman Studio* for a screen test where she met the film crew . . . and also Matin Campania, from *Arts in Tune*, the company co-producing the film.

The filming was to be part of a dance festival. Pip looked forward to researching music for her dolphin ballet.

On the way back from the screen test, Pip visited the Fairy Gardens, where she saw sculpted statues of the founders. She decided to commission the sculptor to make her a bucket. He was away, so Pip left a message with the alarming Frances le Fay.

Pip borrowed an encyclopaedia called *Orders of the Fay* from Edgar and also ordered a set from Jonquil Orange of *The Orange Grove* bookshop. On a whim, she enquired about *Grandmother's Sunshine*. Jonquil believed it was a myth but said someone else had asked for it recently. Pip prevaricated, unwilling to admit her family had two copies of such a rare title.

After a return to the fossmere to dance with Jane and work on her dolphin ballet, *Delphine,* Pip went to the Fairy Gardens to finish blocking the ballet. There, she met the Dames with Dogs. Her attempt to use Cat-Morse on the dogs failed. She spotted a mutie . . . a young man with a Scottie dog self. She tried Dog-Morse on an uncooperative black spaniel who was revealed to be Gillan, the mutie's mother. From her time at the fossmere, Pip identified Gillan and her sons as piskies.

Gillan recognised Pip from her role in the cult film *The House of Heriot,* in which she had starred with Alain Barfleur. Finding Gillan hard work, Pip left, but Gillan made her a re-markable offer.

Book Five, the one you are about to read, begins as Pip makes a failed attempt to visit *over there,* leaves Sydney, and travels to Delphinium Island.

The story continues . . .

PART ONE. *IN TRANSIT*

April 2022

Chapter One. Rasputin

Pippin Pearmain slipped out of the guesthouse a full fifteen minutes before she and her agent, Magda Saxer, were due to leave for the festival at Delphinium Island.

Hoping to stay unobserved, she flitted along the short frontage of the terrace house and nipped round into the courtyard.

Lemon tree. Check. She paused to examine the shrub from a cautious distance. The one back at Lemonwood Cottage had savage tendencies and liked to collude with a sly-eyed gooseberry bush. This one looked cheery and gracious in comparison. Pip approached and stroked a glossy leaf.

"Hm," she observed. "Edgar pees on you at the dead of night. Is that why you look contented?"

She moved on between narrow flower beds bright with late-season petunias and autumn crocus. Honesty raised its coin-shaped seed cases above the display. It was an odd mixture, but the colours harmonised.

A few more paces brought Pip within reach of her objective, a white-painted wooden gate. She'd used that gate this morning at around half-past-six. Edgar Treadwell, the kindly host of the guesthouse, had escorted her through and delivered her to her young friend Ardal who had stood back respectfully while she mounted Fimber the pony. Riding his own bay Indi, he'd taken her to Fosscot to enjoy her ballet practice with Jane.

Ballet in fairyland. What better way was there to start the day?

I must have been an excellent person in a past life to deserve all this. Or maybe I don't deserve it, and someone loves me anyway.

Ardal had fetched her back in time to hand her into Edgar's keeping.

"All reet then, lass?" Edgar spoke like a stage Yorkshireman, although he'd been born in Merimbula.

"Perfectly," she'd assured him.

He'd taken her small hand in his large one and they'd stepped through the gate into the cool of an April Sydney morning.

Since then, she'd had breakfast with Magda and Edgar and his wife, Joan, and she'd readied herself for the next stage of her adventure. That would have less to do with riding and dancing and more to do with a return to stage and film for the first time in more than a decade.

I'm not scared.

There really was nothing to be scared of. For almost fifty years she'd been a performer who danced, observed, reacted, and spoke as directors required and scripts dictated. Performing had been kind to her. So had her acquisition of an intelligent and reassuring agent whose business decisions and financial acumen had steered her cosily through life.

So what if she'd not had a role in years? Her new agent had broken the drought. Performing was like riding a bike.

Pip backtracked a bit from that idea. She hadn't ridden a bike in more years than she could remember.

Performing was like climbing a rope and squealing at a whistle-register pitch.

She's done both of those the week before.

Pip put out her hand and brushed the wooden gate. It felt smoothly splinter-free, sturdy and faintly damp from the dew. She allowed her hand to glide over the uprights and onto the wooden latch.

You can do it. You've seen Edgar unfasten it.

She took hold of the latch and opened it easily.

*If I step through into over there and it closes behind me . . . what
if I can't open it from the other side?*

She smiled.

*I'll wait for someone, maybe Felicity Dark, to come by. Or I could
go to the castle.*

She pictured herself walking up to the arched wooden door
of the castle, grasping the iron ring in both hands, lifting it,
and letting it fall back against the door with a hollow boom.

What ho within!

Who goes there?

It's me.

Who's me?

*Pippin Picotee Pearmain. I need someone to open the gate and let
me back into Sydney.*

It would be that easy. One of the courtfolk who lived there
would greet her courteously and let her through.

Pip stepped through the gate and closed it behind her with
a click.

To her disappointment, the castle was not in sight. Neither
was the bridge, or the flat greensward where she had danced
to Edgar's mouth organ on her first Sydney morning.

She was in someone's garden. Late tomatoes drooped on
yellowed plants. A rake leaned on the fence, and an enormous
cat glowered at her from his seat on an upturned stone urn.
He was a monumental grey tabby with eyes the hue of green
stained glass and a bi-coloured nose, striped in pink and
black. That feature should probably have seemed cute, but it
looked menacing instead, as if she'd caught the cat halfway
through morphing from one colour to another.

There are things humans are not meant to see.

Pip liked cats. She lived with three of them and had lately
met an interesting fourth called Patchwork Norah. This cat,
though —

"Hello, Master Tom," she said. He was clearly a tom.

The monstrous feline opened his mouth and yodelled at

her.

"All right." Pip made patting down motions in the air. "I beg your pardon."

The intelligent eyes gave her a malevolent look. *I beg your pardon*, Sir. The voiceless words came to her clearly, full of contempt.

Pip stiffened her spine. So, the beast spoke Cat-Morse, just like her three feline friends at home. She said, "I'll have you know I live with two of your sort. And another one who was touched by a guardian. And they're all a good deal better-mannered than you are."

Your point?

"My point is—" Pip paused. She knew more or less what her point was, but at that moment she became aware of a man standing silently not far from her left elbow.

He cleared his throat. "May I help you?"

Pip turned her attention to him. He was about forty, she thought, dressed in blue overalls with a logo on the pocket. He had blue eyes that almost matched the overalls and hair the colour of fallen oak leaves.

Not half bad.

"I don't know," she said. "Are you a fay?"

He frowned.

She realised he was holding a mobile phone with the screen lit up. A voice quacked faintly.

Okay. Mobile phones didn't work on the other side of the gates where Ardal and Jane lived, and where Edgar had friends. Ergo . . .

Pip looked about with more attention. An electric pruner dangled from the man's other hand.

He might be fay, but if so, he lives human. It didn't work. I really am still on the human side of the gates.

She emitted a sharp, short huff of air. "Sorry. Your cat disconcerted me. I came through the gate there. I hoped I was going somewhere else."

She'd known it wouldn't work, but she'd had to have a go.

The man raised the phone and spoke into it. "Hold on a bit. I have a situation."

Pip bristled. "I'm not a situation. Your cat—"

His frown upended into a rueful smile. "Not my cat." He added, "Thank goodness."

Seconded, the cat said nastily.

"Whose is he then?"

"He lives with my cousin a few streets over. Raphael Angelus."

"Doesn't look very angelic to me."

"Not the cat. The cat's name is Rasputin."

"What's he doing here?"

"Spying on me. Probably."

Is that so? Pip asked the cat, electing to use silent mode. The bloke with the pruner already seemed to think she was daft.

That's for me to know.

Humph. You'd better run home. Animal Control might put you in the pound.

The cat said quite explicitly what he'd do if Animal Control made the attempt. He flashed his fangs for emphasis. They were long enough to make a vampire weep with envy.

Pip switched her gaze back to the man. "Sorry to have bothered you. I'll go now."

"Go where?"

"Back the way I came. I've been staying at the guesthouse. I'm going to Delphinium Island to star in a film."

"Oh." He added, "This is not my house, you know. I don't live here. I'm Gabe."

"Gabe what?"

"Angelus."

Pip found her lips moving as she put the names together. "Raphael Angelus. Gabe Angelus. Gabe as in Gabriel?"

"I'm afraid so."

Pip said, "Why would you be afraid so? That's a splendid

pair of names. Do you have brothers called Michael and Uriel?"

"My cousins," he said.

"Does Rasputin spy on them too?"

I do not.

Why not?

They work in a hardware shop.

"I don't know," Gabe said. "They've never mentioned it."

Pip gave him her best smile. "Thanks," she said, in a general sort of way. She turned and let herself back into the guesthouse courtyard. A glance behind her showed man and cat still staring at her. The man slowly raised the phone to his ear. The cat sneered.

Pip scuttled back around the front of the guesthouse just in time to see Magda descending the shallow steps.

"There you are," her agent said unnecessarily.

"Here I am," Pip agreed.

"Good. Thought you'd flitted."

Pip considered saying she never flitted, but she remembered she had — once. Once was enough.

"Are we ready?" she asked instead.

"Just about." Magda led the way out to the street. "Our transport should be along about — now."

Chapter Two. "About That Book."

Pip and Magda travelled to Delphinium Island in a wonderfully painted van. It belonged to *Arts in Tune*, and was driven by Matin Campania, who had been at *Diamond Spellman Studio* when Pip did her screen test.

The playwright, Humphrey Carpenter-Rivers, of whom she'd never heard prior to the day of the test, had written the part of Solace in *Half-Life of the Lost* with Pip in mind.

He'd done it twenty-five years ago, when Pip's career had been managed by Sullivan Gilbert.

Had Sully known about that role?

Pip didn't ask. She'd loved and trusted Sully to do her best for them both, and as far as she knew, Sully always had. Surely if Sully had known of a plum part written especially for her client and friend, she would have mentioned it and made sure Pip was attached to the production. Unless, Pip thought, it had been a love job.

Sully had never approved of love jobs. One of her favourite mantras had been *If you do something for nothing, you get nothing. Gifts, favours, nice things, sweet surprises and such are fine, but being asked to work for nothing? Never.*

The last job Sully had got for Pip had been a rare slip-up on Sully's part. She'd been losing her sharp business acumen by then, and she'd forgotten to specify all expenses paid. Pip had been paid for her part in *The Girl in the Frame,* but she'd had to visit a gallery day after day, and the costs had mounted up.

At least an up-front fee had been negotiated. The first offer had been a percentage of the cinema profits after all expenses.

The thing had gone direct to video, so that was a bullet

dodged.

Half-Life of the Lost would have been written long before *The Girl in the Frame*, but if the final offer had been poor, Sully might never even have put it to Pip.

On the other hand, Aberdeen Diamond from the studio had stated the play was insufficiently mainstream to fly in the nineties, which was why it was available for a joint venture between *Diamond Spellman* and *Arts in Tune*. Maybe it had never got past the initial approaches.

The fact that it was to be filmed during a dance festival in which some of the cast and crew were involved seemed daft to Pip. It sounded a recipe for a spectacular disaster, but Matin seemed sure it would work.

Even if it didn't, Pip had been assured she'd still get paid and yes, all expenses beyond the strictly personal would be covered. Pip understood that meant food and accommodation, travel, and anything connected with the film. However, if she visited a high-end jeweller and purchased a diamond ring, that would be her private expense, even if she wore it on-screen.

Ten days filming an arty play about a woman in a coma, among co-stars who had scripts though she had to adlib, while a dance festival thundered around them. What could possibly go wrong?

Yet Magda had accepted the offer.

Pip had never known much about Magda Quest Saxer until about two weeks earlier. She'd had a vague impression of someone who used to manage artists and artists' models . . . and who owned a gallery in Western Australia. She thought Sully might have mentioned her a few times. Magda said they'd been good friends, and she had surely known Sully very well.

Though Magda was outspoken and older than anyone else Pip knew, she was disposed to trust her as she had trusted

Sully.

Pip trusted few people. In the decade since she'd left Delmsford after her mother and Sully died in the same week, she'd lived alone in Jellico Bay. She'd made her home at Lemonwood Cottage, at first with the original cat, Kittisack. Later, they'd been joined by Kittisack's apprentice, Amberjill.

A chance meeting with her cousins Jan and Lupin had offered renewed family contact, but Lupin had died soon after and now only Jan, her daughter Clarkia, and Pip herself remained of the Laurel-Pearmain-de-Leon family.

Clarkia was currently cat-sitting with Kittisack and Amberjill, and the odd pottery being Lupin had made and which Pip knew as Lupin's cat, while grieving the abrupt end of her romance with a duplicitous partner.

Jan was presumably deep in writing her third novel under the pen name Juniper Gin.

Pip was on her way to her first acting role in over a decade, organised by a new agent who was older than she was.

What could possibly go wrong?

Just about anything could go wrong, in Pip's experience. Her last-minute attempt to pay a solo visit *over there* was an interesting case in point. If she'd managed to get through to the castle, she might have been tempted to explore. Maybe it was just as well she'd met the Angelic Gabriel and the not-angelic Rasputin instead.

Rasputin was undoubtedly a fay cat of the same ilk as Kittisack, Amberjill, and Patchwork Norah. How many of the creatures were there wandering around on the human side of the gates? And why? Whyever didn't they stay in the warm and welcoming ambiance of *over there*?

She resolved to put the matter to Edgar and Joan next time she saw them.

Magda, wrapped as usual in her lavishly embroidered shawl, said, abruptly, "About that book."

Chapter Three. *Grandmother's Sunshine*

"Which book?" Pip honestly didn't know, because they'd discussed more than one—several, if she counted the seven volumes of The Orders of the Fay as separate titles. She'd also acquired a new book, Orders of Field and Forest, as a gift quite recently.

"*Grandmother's Sunshine*," Magda said. "May I look at the photos again?"

Pip put away thoughts of yodelling cats and disarming men in overalls and fossicked in her messenger bag. She extracted her phone. "I think they're in the gallery," she said.

Magda flicked and tapped about until she found the five photographs Clarkia had taken of the book and sent upon Pip's request.

"Cover, frontispiece, and three interior spreads," Pip said.

Clarkia had done a good job, with each page straight and in focus . . . not such a simple job with a book, although this one had a sewn spine and opened out flat.

Pip didn't need to look at the photos to know what Magda would see. *Grandmother's Sunshine*, with its rhymes and gentle stories, was a dearly loved part of her childhood, something shared with her largely vanished family.

She'd almost given it to a young friend, once, but after being snubbed by Angie's mother, she'd put it away and never shown it to anyone else till now.

"Tell me about it," Magda ordered.

"I already did." Actually, she wished she hadn't. She'd kept quiet about it for a quarter century, so what imp had made her break that silence now?

Magda said, "I heard you prevaricating with Jonquil Orange. You told me you have it. You told her you'd heard about it from relatives. I want to know which version of the story is true."

"Both, obviously," Pip said, but baiting Magda was probably not sensible, so she clarified, "As I told you, I don't know much about the books. You can see the inscription on this copy . . . *From Grandmother Aster to her sweet Cammie.* I never thought to ask about it until my grandparents and parents were gone, but Jan—my younger cousin—said she asked, and Little Nanna Laurel told her she remembered Callie. She was her great-grandmother."

"This name is Cammie, though." Magda air-tapped the screenshot of the frontispiece.

"That's right. Jan said Little Nanna told her Callie had a sister called Cammie. There's supposed to be a photo of them somewhere, but neither of us knows where. It mightn't even exist anymore. Little Nanna might have remembered it from when she was young."

Magda said, "Are you implying you and your cousin are descended from two different sisters?"

"No, we're both descended from Little Nanna, and she was descended from Callie." Pip frowned, counting on her fingers. "If Callie was Little Nanna's great granny, that made her Little Mum and Aunt Helen's great-great granny and Jan's, Lupin's and my great-great-great granny. I think."

"That sounds right," Magda said.

"And I think that means Cammie was our great-great-great-great aunt, because you add on one extra great for an aunt or uncle. Probably. So she wasn't a direct ancestor."

"Not unless she and her sister had children with brothers,

which would make both sisters your three-times-great grand-mothers," Magda said.

"Gosh, I hope not!" Pip screwed up her face and began to hum. She disliked the idea, but it might explain a few things about the Laurel-Pearmain-de-Leon families.

"It wouldn't matter as long as the resulting descendants didn't have children with one another," Magda said.

Pip went on humming.

Magda poked her. "Stop that."

Pip broke off. "However it happened, we ended up with both copies of the book. Mine's the Cammie one, and Lupin and Jan had the Callie one."

"Any idea why?"

"I didn't even know where they came from until Jan told me a couple of weeks ago. The only reason I can think of is that Lupin was four years older than I am, and maybe Little Nanna's grandmother . . . no, that wouldn't work. Maybe our great-grandmother gave her grandmother's book to Lupin be-cause she was the first child born in our generation. But that won't work either, because Little Mum and Aunt Helen had the books when they were children."

"It could have been the same deal," Magda said. "Which was the elder sister?"

"No idea," Pip said. She added, "They were fraternal twins, and Little Nanna Laurel had them at home. I know that, because she was a bit annoyed when Jan went to hospital to have Clarkia."

Magda said, "Apart from the inscription from Grand-mother Aster, there's no more information. Is there a page with a publication date and publishing details? Or even an author's name? Or an artist's?"

"No. I'd have had Clarkia photograph it if there had been." She leaned back. "Why are you interested in my ancestors? I wish I'd asked more about them, but I didn't, and it's too late now."

"Not necessarily. Your mother and aunt were probably born in the twentieth century — right?"

"Yes. The year *Lenten Rose* sank."

"Therefore, your grandmother was a nineteenth century birth."

"They both were."

"That means their records will probably be available through Link-Me."

Pip tilted her head in question.

"That's a social platform set up back in the noughties to reunite friends who've lost touch. It's evolved, though, and now it has a genealogy component. It lists births and marriages prior to nineteen hundred, but it has a collaborative feature so people working on the same family line can build on one another's discoveries."

"You could use it to find your mother," Pip suggested.

"There's too little to go on. I know my father's dates, but he and Francine were never married. I don't have her full name, or her address, or even a date of birth. She looks about the same age as my father in the photo, but her cloche hat makes it difficult to see her face in detail. Besides, if she did have sylvan ancestry, she might have been much older than she looked."

Like you and Jillian Jules, Sam and Oash.

"Isn't her name on your birth certificate?" Pip asked.

"She didn't register me. She went home to pave the way with her parents — so she said — and stepped out of my life forever. When Mum realised she was never coming back, she registered me and put her name down as my parent."

Pip understood the woman Magda called Mum was in fact her paternal grandmother.

"Also, there is not likely to be anyone else building on my family. My father was an only child and so was Mum. I don't know who my grandfathers were, and I suspect Quest is a matrilineal name."

Pip started humming again. Magda's family had so nearly died out, but her late marriage and the birth of a daughter and grandchildren had got it going again. If she remembered correctly, Magda's daughter, Marianna Mackenzie, had three sons, so it would be unusual if at least one of them failed to provide an heir for the Quest Saxers.

There were three of you Laurel-Pearmain-de-Leon girls. Only Jan had a child, and Clarkia seems unlikely —

"What has this to do with *Grandmother's Sunshine?*" she asked, to drown her regretful mind-chatter.

"I thought, by working back from your grandmother — what was her name?"

Pip decided Magda meant the one concerned with the book. "Nanna Laurel. Her first name was Schizanthus."

Magda looked up from the phone. "Really?"

"It's a flower name."

"And a huge piece of luck. It's so uncommon as a first name you won't keep running into doppelgangers. Think if she'd been Mary Laurel! What was her original surname?"

Pip opened her mouth to respond then closed it again, realising she had no idea. In fact, she didn't know Little Nanna Pearmain's original name, either. Her first name had been Picotee, which was why Pip had it as a middle name. Little Mum's name had been Rose Guelder Laurel.

"No idea," she admitted, since Magda was obviously waiting.

"If you know her birthday, you could probably find her anyway."

With Schizanthus as a name, that seemed likely, but Pip still didn't understand Magda's insistence. She supposed it would be nice to know, but who else would be interested, aside from — possibly — Jan? And if Jan had been interested in genealogy she'd have done all this already.

Maybe she has.

Aside from debuting a late-blooming career as a novelist and keeping Lupin company during her last few months of life, Pip had little idea of how Jan had filled her time over the past decade, or even before.

They'd been as close as sisters once.

"From working back from your grandmother, you might find the identity of Grandmother Aster," Magda persisted.

"Possibly, but why bother? I get that she gave a book to each of her grandchildren, and the books eventually came down to Lupin and Jan and me, but knowing who she was won't give us anything useful. There's no knowing when the book was published. If these copies were bought in the late seventeen hundreds, or early nineteenth century, say, they might have been printed years before. Why on earth does it matter to you?"

Magda pulled her shawl around her. "It doesn't, of course."

But Pip saw it did.

"Magda. You're not suggesting you and I could be related, are you?"

Magda looked genuinely surprised. "That's very unlikely. I'd just like to know the provenance of those books."

"Why?"

Magda thumbed through the gallery on Pip's phone and opened one of the spreads. She enlarged it several times so just a detail filled the screen. "Look."

Pip peered at it. She was familiar enough with the book to recognise the page from the small section of picture. Perhaps coincidentally, it was the illustration for the rhyme Jan had quoted on the day she'd visited Pip to give her Lupin's cat.

Pip quoted it now. "Out of the cobwebs, a piece of the sun, from thistles and velvet are kitten-cats spun." She examined the head and shoulders of a cat. Clarkia had photographed the page in lamplight, so there was a yellowish glow that faded at the edges of the paper. The cat was cream and brown with hints of purple in the shadows under its chin. The hair looked real enough to stroke.

She noted for the first time that the cat looked very like Kittisack — but all seal point Siamese had the same general colouring, so she didn't attach anything important to that.

"I looked. What about it? It's a lovely picture, but I've known it all my life, just the way I've known the pictures of *Ironbark Joe* and *Prince Pommier*, the apple tree prince."

Magda said, "Ironbark Joe — the bullocky? From the book by Joseph Miller?"

"Yes. Big Pop had a signed first edition — I expect Jan still has it."

"I don't know the other one," Magda said, frowning.

"It's a fairy tale, but not by Anderson or the Grimms. The pictures are line drawings, not paintings, and it was for older children or adults — a kind of romance. That one came from Little Pop Pearmain. I think it belonged to his mother."

Magda said, "Do you still have it?"

Pip put her phone to sleep and slid it into her messenger bag as she sidestepped adroitly. "I still have most of my old books." She hoped Magda wasn't going to interview her about every book in her home library.

"Would your cousin photograph that one for me?"

"I expect so, but why? You're an agent, not a book dealer, but it can't be idle interest."

"It isn't." Magda folded her hands and apparently decided to come clean.

CHAPTER FOUR. THE EAVESDROPPER

"You know I have an art gallery," Magda said.

"You told me you had one in the seventies."

"I still have it. *Magdala Gallery* at Tom Cat Hill. I have represented artists' models for years — which was how I came to know Peter P and his family — and also Judit Creed. She used to work with Peter sometimes. They had amazing chemistry, but they were simply friends.

"Aside from keeping models safe from bigger sharks than I am, I also showcase retrospectives — either on a one-off basis or, occasionally, exclusively. I have fewer artists and models on my books nowadays, because so many of the modern ones do installation or online work, but one of my interests is illustration. Book illustration used to be seen as a lesser artform than fine art and portraiture, but I've always maintained it can be every bit as brilliant. I've had displays of children's book illustrations — mostly nineteenth century — involving artists who died before nineteen-thirty. I have a few living illustrators — I'd have made a deal with Pen Inkersoll — Panda's daughter-in-law — except that she's contracted to Thymelines. I thought I was familiar with most, if not all, the topflight illustrators of the nineteenth century and with some of the earlier ones, but I can't place these, and, dammit, I should be able to." She appeared to look for the pictures.

"I put my phone away," Pip said.

"If I could find the artist's identity and ascertain whether he — or she — passed on more than seventy years ago — "

"Must have done," Pip said.

"Not necessarily. If an artist was working at the age of twenty, it would be possible for illustrations done in eighteen sixty-two to be still under copyright protection via the lifetime plus seventy rule."

Pip recalled asking Matin Campania about the copyright status of the music she wanted to use for the dolphin ballet she had choreographed. She wanted to buy his wife's first album and interrogate her about new music.

She looked up the body of the van and accidentally caught his gaze in the rear-view mirror. He looked—interested.

He's been eavesdropping.

She knew she couldn't be too angry, as she'd always rationalised her own listening-in habit by thinking anyone speaking in a public place to a visible audience was fair game.

Nevertheless, she wasn't too pleased with Magda for raising the subject in the van, considering she'd said she wouldn't mention Pip's possession of the rare title to others . . . or did she just mean she wouldn't mention it to collectors and booksellers?

On the other hand, what could he hear? He was up the front, and they were seated in the body of the van. There was considerable traffic and road noise as they drove out of the city. He shouldn't have heard more than a murmur.

To test it out, she said, at the same volume she'd used to talk with Magda, "Mister Campania, your wife is a musician. That must keep her busy?"

His reflected eyes crinkled slightly, and he raised his voice to answer. "Indeed it does. She's also a portraitist and an illustrator."

Pip recalled that he'd said his wife would like to paint her. "Oh? Would I know any of her illustration work?"

"She hasn't done many titles yet, but you might know the series called *Jacaranda Journey*."

Magda came to full alert.

"So that's why your name is familiar! You're Tamzin Campania's husband! I met her at the 2020 Vision exhibition — and you were there, too. Why the hell didn't I recognise you at *Diamond Spellman?*"

"You were talking with Jasper mostly, and besides — I was out of context."

Magda harumphed. "Must be getting old." She turned to Pip. "I'm going to move up and grill Master Campania while I've got him trapped in the van. He might prove elusive once we get to the island."

She gathered her shawl around her and moved up to the front passenger seat, leaving Pip to blow out her cheeks in relief.

Half an hour of intensive questioning from Magda Saxer was more than she'd wanted. What did it matter exactly how old *Grandmother's Sunshine* was? She understood what Magda meant about the illustrations being out of copyright and therefore free to reproduce or to repurpose, but the books weren't Magda's to use.

Maybe it was academic interest.

She wondered idly if other people felt that way about her when she was on the quest for information. Probably.

She mentally apologised to Gillan and Zennor St Ives, whom she'd grilled in the Fairy Gardens the day before.

No wonder Gillan had been grumpy.

Yet Gillan had turned out to be unexpectedly gracious.

Pip slid her hand back into her messenger bag and snagged the card Gillan had left for her in a hamper of goodies. They'd met that day for the first time at the Fairy Gardens when Gillan, in her secondary guise as the spaniel bitch called Lady Velvet, had been minding her own business and watching the Dames and dogs enjoying a social gathering.

Pip had endeavoured to engage the seeming dog in a Dog-Morse experiment. She communicated with the three cats who shared her cottage in Cat-Morse, so why wouldn't it work on dogs?

After some prompting from her amused son, the disgruntled Lady Velvet had morphed into the equally grumpy Gillan St Ives.

Pip had been surprised, but not shocked. She'd seen that kind of transformation twice before and was nearly sure she'd seen it again that very day. She wondered if the other people at the park noticed. Maybe it was just an accepted thing that everyone knew, and no one mentioned? Or maybe their eyes and brains had rewritten the sight into something more believable.

After a bit of verbal jousting, and an explanation of why what she was trying wouldn't work on Lady Velvet, she'd left the mother and son and gone off to work on her ballet choreography. The hamper Gillan had left for her was a total surprise.

Pip had already drunk the lemon barley from the flask and eaten the two tarts. She'd cut up and shared the apples with Jane and Trae at the fossmere that morning. The bunch of marigolds had come along with her in their vase, standing in a bucket donated by Edgar Treadwell.

It was a nice sturdy bucket, painted with a quaint fairy-tale scene showing two green-faced trolls dressed as humans. In fact, they were wearing the same clothing Edgar and Joan favoured.

Must be a custom job, like those mocked-up Wanted posters, or those silly animations that let you put family faces onto dancing reindeer.

The bucket was much nicer than those, and he'd said she could keep it as a souvenir of her stay at the guesthouse.

Edgar had been so kind, what with lending her the encyclopaedia—which he'd allowed her to bring to the festival—playing for her dancing practice, escorting her to the fossmere, and giving her the bucket. She poked it with her toe, releasing a waft of the odd scent of marigolds.

The rest of the hamper contents were a silver puppy charm, now strung on the silver cord and hanging on her wrist, the card itself, a silky length of printed cloth she thought might make a wall-hanging or a bed-throw, and the pretty little book called *Orders of Field and Forest*.

Safe from Magda's scrutiny, Pip re-read the card with Gillan's astonishing offer.

She claimed she wasn't being altruistic, but it was still a generous undertaking.

If you still want to try your ingenious Dog-Morse experiment on a fay dog, rather than wasting your time on clueless standard dogs and uncooperative muties, I suggest you obtain a puppy and work with her — bitches are more amenable, despite what my husband says — from an impressionable age. If you would like to do this, let me know and I will source a suitable puppy for you.

Gillan had promised it would cost Pip nothing to obtain the dog. Obviously, it would need food and shelter, but she already fed two of the three cats — Lupin's cat didn't require feeding — so what would one more small animal matter? Like Kittisack and Amberjill, a fay puppy would have perfect health. Gillan had even undertaken not to pester her for updates, although she'd said they would be welcome.

She'd listed four possible types of dog — small and delicate harlequins, medium-sized and calm hollies, enthusiastic and chaotic heather hoonds, and the discreet shadowhonds. This last type sounded sinister, although Gillan said they had good manners.

Should I even consider it?

Pip put the card back in her bag and extracted her trusty feint-ruled writing pad. She'd had it for decades. It had once borne minutes from her brief stint as minute-taker for the Delmsford Flower Committee. Cousin Lupin had dealt with those by ripping them off in her brisk fashion and flinging them into a bucket on the afternoon tearoom at the Flower

Show. Lupin had been dying, but she hadn't seemed ill.

What was wrong with her? No one had said.

The bulk of the pad was taken up with Pip's bucket list — a lovingly tended list of buckets she remembered, done in her miniature writing which was no bigger than typescript. She planned to expand this enterprise into a custom-made album with photos, drawings, scans, and supporting content. She could hardly wait. Before then, though, she'd add the troll bucket she'd acquired from Edgar. The Treadwell Bucket, she would style it. That sounded rather like an archaeological treasure dug up from some distant historical site.

What a nice man Edgar was, despite his growling voice and alarming size. Joan was lovely, too, but Pip had spent more time with Edgar.

More recently, the pad had acquired writing in other hands. After learning of the bucket list, Jan and Lupin had traded their own secrets, writing them down for Pip to consider at leisure. She'd got a new secret from Zach Rowan when he'd taken her sailing on the yacht *Tulpenmanie*. The feint-ruled pad was turning into a regular confessional and repository for other people's secrets.

Pip briefly contemplated tearing out the bits she hadn't written, but that seemed disrespectful to Lupin who had given her such an amazing gift in her Vouch-Safe Experience.

The next few pages after that were taken up with choreography for her ballet, *Delphine,* and the stand-alone scene she thought of as *Queen of the Clowder.* In that one, a playful tribe of cats celebrated their ageing queen, who was forgetful and sometimes clumsy, but whom they all loved and supported.

Pip was aware this small ballet was self-indulgent, and that she would probably never get to stage it, but if she ever did, she would dance the queen.

Maybe I can do it when I launch my final career as the dancing centenarian . . .

If she lived that long.

She had another thirty-four years to get through first.

The thought was unexpectedly liberating. All her new ideas and potential projects had been crowding in on her, but if she could manage another thirty-four years, surely she could fit them in.

Magda had.

According to her, she'd been born after her father died of the Spanish flu, which must have been around 1920. Pip had no reason to disbelieve her.

I could look up Magdala Gallery on find-me.

She was about to hit up her phone for a good reciprocal nose about in Magda's affairs when she remembered her more urgent purpose.

She unclipped her green pen and turned back the pages of ballet notes to reveal a new page.

At the top of it, she wrote —

Pros and Cons of Accepting a Fay Puppy from Gillan St Ives

CHAPTER FIVE. PROS AND CONS

Pip underlined it three times for emphasis, then pulled out the card and used it as a straight edge to rule the page into two columns.

Pros.

I get to find out if Dog-Morse will work.

A dog might be more active company than the cats. It could come along when I walk on the beach.

The cats did go with her occasionally, but they tended to flit off on their own tangents, re-joining her much later at home.

She frowned, tapping the paper with her pen. Surely there were more pros than that? The Dames with Dogs members she'd met at the Fairy Gardens had all seemed lovingly engaged with their canine companions.

She considered the possibility of joining the Dames if and when she got a pup, but she decided it would never work. She lived in a different state. But—maybe there was a chapter in north-eastern Tasmania?

Must ask . . . um . . . Caddy. Pandora's her sister, so she'll know how to contact her.

That's if I decide to accept Gillan's offer.

She wrote the heading for the other side of the column.

Cons.

The cats might object to a puppy, and it is their home too.

But—they didn't mind Kakao.

But—Kakao isn't an actual dog. He's Jamie's manifestation.

Dogs are good company, but they're always there. Cats are able to entertain themselves or vanish for hours.

Training a puppy would take time and patience.

If it didn't like me, I'd have to decide what to do about that.

If I get more roles after Half-Life of the Lost, *I would be away from home more often.*

But – Clarkia would dog-sit for me.

Or . . . would she? Jan's daughter Clarkia was taking refuge at Lemonwood Cottage after discovering her boyfriend had a family he returned to whenever he was away on business. He'd wanted to talk about the situation, but Clarkia emphatically didn't, so she was hiding out at Pip's place under an assumed name. Since Pip had never met the boyfriend and didn't even know his name, and since she'd had no contact with Clarkia for about twenty years prior to their recent reunion, it seemed unlikely the man would know her cottage existed, let alone where it was.

Clarkia had shown herself obliging in the matter of photographing *Grandmother's Sunshine*, and Jan said she was sensible and capable. Yet would she really want to spend several weeks a year holed up in someone else's cottage minding three cats and a dog?

Even if I do find out about Dog-Morse, exactly what good will that do? Knowing Cat-Morse has just enhanced my reputation for being odd. It's fun, and it helps me to get along with the cats, but – Mister Nasty Paws Rasputin is one argument against it.

According to Gillan, ordinary dogs wouldn't understand it, even if I did learn to use it. Well, that's her opinion. She'd never heard of it until I told her, so what does she know about the subject?

I could teach it to Clarkia . . .

Oops. That belonged in the Pros column. Pip remembered suggesting to her cousin that if she enjoyed looking after Kittisack and Amberjill, she might start a pet-sitting business called *Purrs and Fur* which would work well with her current occupation as a beta-reader.

Whether she'd consider it probably depended on who got

the house she'd occupied with her boyfriend. He wouldn't want it. Pip assumed he'd be either mending bridges with his original girlfriend and children or possibly in hiding from both women. Maybe that was why he wanted to talk to Clarkia. Maybe Original Girlfriend had thrown him out.

Clarkia wouldn't take him back. No matter how sorry he was, he had lied to her for four years.

But would Clarkia be able to buy him out of the house? Had they even owned it? If not, house-and-pet sitting might be a useful way to get accommodation and to get paid to stay in it.

A puppy would disrupt my life. It would need more hands-on affection than a cat. Acquiring it would be a deliberate action. The cats just – arrived.

Pip sighed. That was the real con. She'd pleased herself for so much of her life. Sully's clever management and her parents' sensible investments had meant she made enough to live comfortably in between jobs. Apart from her offer to help Jan with the logistics after Lupin's passing—an offer Jan hadn't needed—she couldn't remember when she'd last put someone else's needs and desires ahead of her own.

Agreeing to let Clarkia stay didn't count, as it was all to her own advantage.

Aside from giving a treasured bucket to Jan for Lupin's last repose, which also didn't count as it eased her guilt and sadness, the last generous impulse she'd had must have been— oh, Lord—back in 1997, when she'd tried to give her copy of *Grandmother's Sunshine* to Angie Blake. Angie had loved the book when Pip read it to her when she minded the child for her mother, Alison. That had been her own idea. She and Angie, despite the forty or so years between them, had shared an enjoyment of dancing, stories, rhymes, and messing about in the garden. They'd both liked the Butterfly Princess products, and they'd sung silly songs together. Angie liked to draw, so they'd sat together playing Squiggles.

She'd impulsively offered to lend her book to Angie. Then, when Alison demurred, she'd offered it free and clear.

Alison had closed her down but had allowed her to give Angie a new book instead.

Things had never been quite the same between them, and not long after, the Blakes had moved away, leaving no forwarding address. She'd never heard from them again.

Maybe that event had killed her generosity.

If so, she ought to be heartily ashamed. Alison had every right to refuse to take an heirloom. Or had she'd seen it as a tattered old book that might have silverfish?

It's not tattered.

Despite its age, *Grandmother's Sunshine* was in excellent vintage condition, slightly bumped and foxed, but adhering firmly to its spine. Its thick pages still had their integrity.

Little Mum had said it was made of flax and rags, so the paper was acid-free and wouldn't crumble.

Pip recalled she had had an impulse to give her heaven and earth ring to Zach's girlfriend Jisinia while sailing on *Tulpenmanie*, but she'd changed her mind. The ring was now hidden in a niche behind the falls of the fossmere, giving her a physical link to the loveliest place she knew.

She wasn't sad she no longer had the ring in her possession. She knew exactly where it was. She could recover it if she chose.

And — she faced it — she was glad Alison Blake had refused to let Angie keep the book. It was a family heirloom, and it should stay in the family . . . what there was of it.

Maybe Clarkia would find love again and have a precious child.

Two, Pip decided. One for each copy of the book.

She might not even need to find love. Some people had babies via a known or unknown doner father, and it could work beautifully. She recalled that Mama Tam, the water maid who was part of the fossmere family, had six children. Her three boys with her husband Liam Dancey may have been born out of mutual love, but her first three had been fathered by men Tam chose especially. Her criteria for baby-fathers had evidently been all-round excellence, and having met Team Tam as they referred to themselves, Pip thought she'd picked well. Liam, far from being jealous that the other men had been chosen first, was quite smug because he, as he told Pip at their meeting, had given her three fine sons, yes, and wed her before he laid her down! He had an ambition to be known by an odd term that apparently meant Father of millions. His eldest son, Finn, was already expecting a child with his wife, so Liam was assured of a new generation.

I should tell Clarkia about Tam. Maybe she could look for excellent breeding material instead of someone to love . . . that nice Gabriel Angelus would do . . . The idea startled her into laughter.

She could just hear herself advising her little-known cousin to take a leaf out of the book of a woman who was — well, Tam could never live in the human world.

Tam would never want to.

PART TWO. DELPHINIUM ISLAND

April 2022

Chapter One. Welcome to Dance in Tune

Delphinium Island, Pip discovered when they arrived, really was an island, connected to the mainland via a causeway. A brightly painted banner arched overhead, proclaiming *Welcome to Dance in Tune!*

A solid boom-gate barred traffic from crossing the causeway, and Matin paused the van to talk with the guard, or guide, or whatever he was who was checking people in.

Pip expected them to be waved through, since Campania was a festival director, but the guard, clad in a shirt with a huge zigzag saying *Lanners!* with *at Arts in Tune* underneath it gestured for him to pull over.

Pip heard Matin say, "Really?" in an exasperated tone, but he complied.

The guard stuck his head in the window. "Tickets."

"We're providers," Matin said.

"Schedules, then . . . and have you signed the declaration?"

"I wrote the declaration and your father edited and approved it."

The guard moved down the side of the van and opened it to peer at Pip. "Have you signed the declaration, ma'am?"

Pip opened her messenger bag and pulled out the declaration she'd signed that morning. She looked up to hand it to the guard and did a classic double take.

"Zennor?"

The man certainly looked like Zennor St Ives, but he

showed no recognition.

Ah, Pip thought wisely, it must be the other one, Zennor's brother, Mullion, though what he was doing here was beyond her.

"Is your rump very sore?" she asked, injecting sympathy into her voice.

"My —" He frowned.

"Your rump, where that cranky little mixed dog bit you at the Fairy Gardens. You put your paw on his head to discipline him."

Campania and Magda were both peering down the body of the van, but Pip ignored them.

"You were disguised as a black Scottie at the time," she reminded him.

The man stared at her as if she might be an earwig. "I beg your pardon —"

Pip said affably, "I know what I saw, so don't you play the pretended outrage card. I had a conversation with your mum and your brother, although you didn't feature greatly in that. Your mum offered me a dog to train. I don't think she meant you, but I'm willing to try if you are. I'll even allow you to pee on my lemon tree if you want to. Mind, though — the camomile is strictly off limits."

The young man's eyes, which Pip saw were delft blue like his brother's, lit up with unholy glee. "You're Marigold! I heard about you, but I didn't expect to see you here."

Someone cleared his throat and Pip looked beyond Mullion St Ives to see Matin had got out of the van and come to her rescue. Or possibly it was St Ives he was planning to save.

"I'm sure you're enjoying yourselves playing verbal ping pong, but traffic is piling up behind us. Mullion, do us all a favour and just pass us through. Or do I need to get Lady Velvet onto your case?"

"Right away." St Ives clicked his fingers and acquired a

pen from somewhere. He took Pip's declaration and wrote something on it before handing it back. Then he stood away from the van and bowed gravely. "Pass, Providers. Venture forth and provide with pride and derring do."

"Thank you, Gatekeeper," Matin said mildly, and got back into the van.

The boom lifted and he drove through a wide green space towards a swathe of buildings of all sizes, ranging from ranks of what looked like alpine chalets to a vast hall with transparent walls.

"The sound stage is off to the side," he said, pointing. "There's a second one, which will be in use while we're filming. I'll get you some keys presently, and you can choose your accommodation — tent, cabin, chalet, or the share-house or barn . . . but I warn you, if you choose the barn, you'll have to share with Hush — that's our pony, unless she's in the house — my wife's riding horse and probably half a dozen goats."

Pip said, "How do you live with all this going on all the time?"

Matin smiled at her. "It's not all the time, Miss Pearmain. Besides, our house is on the other side of the island, through the trees. It's surprisingly quiet." He added, "Once you've decided where you want to sleep, you can wander around the area. The kitchen and the vans are just warming up, but order anything you want. I can either give you a booklet of vouchers, or a T-shirt or a badge to mark you as providers."

"Do you have shirts in my size?" Pip asked.

"We have shirts in all sizes. They come from a shop called Fairings, which belongs to my friend Otto's mother. She guarantees a perfect fit, or your money back."

"We have to pay for them?" Pip managed to sound outraged.

"No. They're provided, along with food and accommodation. You can keep them to wear at home. That way they act as advertising. You can pick from a lot of different designs. Go to the Icehouse over there and see what takes your fancy."

Pip glanced at Magda, who didn't look like a T-shirt sort of person.

"I think I'll pass on the shirt, but I'll wear a badge," Magda said. "Do you have any objection to sharing a cabin with me, Pippin? It might save time if we can have somewhere to convene without having to make special arrangements."

"I don't mind at all, as long as you don't have an objection to my ballet practice at seven in the morning. I generally dance and exercise for an hour."

Magda looked a little less than enthusiastic.

Matin said, "You can join the *Forevers* for practice, if you like. They'll be limbering up at some point in the fairly early morning. You might also join the *Dads*."

"Who or what are the *Forevers* and the *Dads?*"

Magda said, "The *Forevers* are a dance troupe from Patterdale in Victoria. It's run by the Almaclairs—Gervais, Hamish, and Flori." She glanced at Matin. "I hope you know what you're doing, Master Campania. I've had dealings with that lot."

"Oh?"

"One of my clients lives in the tower where they're based, and I've encountered various bits of the troupe in consequence," she said. "Some of them are his grandchildren . . . or maybe great-grandchildren. I lose track of the generations."

"What about the *Dads?*" Pip asked.

Magda shrugged. "Can't help you there."

Matin said, "The *Dads* are actually a group called *Dad Ballet,* based up the coast at Fiddle Bay. They're a male troupe made up of dancers of mixed ages and backgrounds. I believe they began as a charity act, but the idea took off. They're not necessarily all dads, and they might have a few women members too—"

"Like the Dames with Dogs?" Pip put in.

Magda gave her a funny look.

"One of the Dames told me they could have men as members — if any men wanted to join — because of Pantomime Dames. Maybe the *Dads* do the same thing because of *Principal Boys* . . ." She shrugged. "Oh, never mind."

Matin said, "I have heard of a quartet called *The Odd Gentlemen*. One of the members is a woman. They're not booked for this festival, though. In any case, you will find plenty of people to practise with."

He handed Magda two keys. "Cabin six. And if the *Forevers* give me any trouble, I'll threaten them with you."

Magda gave a dry cackle. "You do that. I, in turn, will threaten them with their grandfather for whom even they have wholesome respect."

Matin said, "Your cases are in your cabin, and I'll tag you in the database so the *Diamond Spellman* contingent know you're here — and so the other actors can find you if necessary. I'll be around if you need anything, and so will my wife, and my wife's foster brothers, whom you seem to know already, Miss Pearmain. Feel free to give those two as much grief as you like." He lifted a hand, turned and merged into a group of people wearing polo shirts with logos.

Magda looked at the keys in her hand. "There's more to that young man than is immediately apparent. Let's find our cabin."

Pip followed her through a maze of buildings, occasionally dodging a goat.

She knew about goats, because Little Pop Laurel had had a pair of milking nannies, but there was something about these creatures that she found disconcerting. They gave her sly-eyed glances that reminded her of the carnivorous gooseberry bush at home at Lemonwood Cottage. They seemed to be calculating her net worth, which they probably measured in treats.

"They're fay goats," Magda said when she ventured to ask their provenance. "I know the type pretty well. Peter P has had a flock for decades."

Pip brightened. "I wonder if Goat-Morse is a thing?"

Magda gave her a baffled look.

Pip explained about Kittisack and Amberjill—and about Lupin's cat, all of whom communicated in Cat-Morse—when they chose. She didn't mention Patchwork Norah, let alone Rasputin.

"What was that you said to the pisky lad who was giving Matin cheek at the gate?" Magda asked when she'd finished.

"About the dog? Or about his rump?"

"Both. Did I understand you to say he's a mutie?"

"You know about those?"

"I can't say I'm on close terms with any, but I certainly know of them. How did you come to meet him?"

Pip explained about Jamie, who had driven her to and from her V-S Experience, and how she'd spotted the St Ives contingent at the Fairy Gardens and tried Dog-Morsing Lady Velvet, who had finally been forced to morph into a woman form to deal with her.

Magda unlocked one of the cabin doors. "You have been busy, Pippin. I was under the impression you were somewhat of a recluse."

"I am," Pip said.

"Yet you flit about *over there* with Edgar, get a hob lad to take you riding, jump off yachts with strange halflings, infiltrate the Dames with Dogs, annoy upstart young men, pester mutie bitches who are minding their own business, flirt with cameramen, and get offered a fay puppy to raise and Dads to dance with."

"Ja. *Und?*"

Magda said, "What's with the cod German?"

Pip recalled that with Magda's small amount of alpenfee blood she might take that as mockery. "Sorry, it's family-speak. Jan and Lupin and I always used to do it when we were young. We caught it from associating with Big Pop de Leon, who had a German friend we called Herr Fischer. At least, I think he was German. I suppose he might have been alpenfee, or Swiss. He made the most incredible cheese called Birnenkäse." She sidled past Magda into the cabin. "Ooh, this is nice. Look! Someone's brought my bucket!"

Chapter Two. The Icehouse

While Magda settled in, choosing a bed and arranging her luggage, Pip went to the Icehouse, which was the huge see-through building. There was a workshop area in the middle, and all kinds of providers, as Matin had termed them, milling about around the walls.

Pip soon found the shirt stall, where she spent a happy half hour bamboozling the very young man minding the display. His nametag said he was Asher Castleby, and he had honest eyes and interesting ears. He gazed at her with apparent fascination as she sorted through piles of shirts. As Matin had said, there were a great many styles and colour combinations to pick from. Pip rarely bought new clothing, because she could still wear things she'd had for years and had no fashion sense anyway. When she did buy something, it was often from a thrift shop or market, and usually because the garment had seemed to call to her, saying *I am yours*.

And *no*, she thought with a sudden smile, *I know that's a fancy. I definitely do not believe in Clothing-Morse. Or not much.*

The shirts on offer were all appealing, so she sought a second opinion from the nice boy.

"What one do you think I should have to prove I'm a provider and get fed, Asher?"

He looked interested instead of merely fascinated. "What's your favourite clothing colour, mistress?"

"Green," Pip said. She decided to let the mistress stand. She was nobody's mistress, but at least he hadn't hit her with the dreaded Ms. She was wearing the rust-coloured divided skirt and blouse Jane's sister Sulane had given her, but she generally did choose green, if it was an option. In fact, she was wearing her green daisy-toed shoes.

"How about patterns? Or do you like plain colours?"

"I like pretty things, so butterflies, or cats or lemons or apples . . . unless you have something with buckets on it. I love buckets."

"This one would suit you." He pulled out a soft green blouse with a drift of pink butterflies over one shoulder, heading towards a spray of what Pip thought was probably apple blossom. "Oh, and there's this as well . . ." With the other hand, and without looking, he snagged a loose-fitting dress with the same design.

Pip said, reluctantly, "I'm only supposed to have a shirt . . ." She brightened. "I could buy the dress. It looks as though it would fit."

A young woman with dark curly hair popped up from somewhere under the table and put her arm around Asher, showing off a gold bracelet with a dangling crystal heart. "It's a nice offer. I should take it if I were you, Ms—"

"Pippin Pearmain, and it's Miss. I'm a provider, apparently."

"I'm Jessie. And seriously, take the offer. Asher doesn't sew much, but his mother is the best embroiderer in the country, and he knows clothes. And he likes ladies, don't you my love? So he won't ever lead you astray. Mind you, I might, if you were up for it."

The lad blushed, and Jessie winked at Pip.

"Leave them here for a few minutes, and I'll get the embroidery done. What are you providing?"

Pip had to think about that. "I'm performing in a film, if that's what you mean."

Jessie nodded. "Ah! You'll be on the list Matin gave us, then. I'll sort something out."

Pip continued her circuit of the Icehouse, wondering if Jessie had just propositioned her. Surely not.

She was beginning to feel overloaded with sounds and impressions when someone put a hand on her shoulder.

She jumped and half turned, but the sweet smell of apricots and bread made her smile with instant recognition. "Tane Pendennis."

"Miss Pippin Pearmain," he responded.

Pip turned to look him over. She'd got to know Jane's father pretty well over the week she'd spent at the fossmere, but then he'd been wearing what he called a pisky kilt and engaged in family activities with his spouse, Jillian Jules, his five children, ranging from Jane in her upper teens to baby Tallien, and an assortment of others connected in ways Pip had trouble remembering. He apparently loved them all, and they loved him. Judging by Jane's age, he was probably over forty, but he didn't look it.

He looked almost unrecognisable in his festival get-up of jeans and a T-shirt. His said *Pisky Waters,* with three wavy lines underneath, which she remembered was the name of his jewellery business. The words, at *Arts in Tune* were embroidered underneath.

She saw how things worked with the providers. Their shirts or badges advertised their own enterprises, and also *Arts in Tune.* She wondered what Jessie would put on hers. *Half-Life of the Lost,* at *Arts in Tune* maybe?

Matin Campania, or whoever advised him, had a good eye for detail, advertising the festival while also allowing for personal preference and personal advertising as well.

"What are you doing here?" she asked Tane. "Jane didn't say anything this morning . . ."

Was it only this morning I was dancing with Jane on the chalk stage?

Tane shrugged. "Did you tell her you were coming here?"

"No . . . it never came up. We were talking about dancing,

mostly."

"She'll be surprised to see you, then—"

"She's here?"

He shook his head. "Not yet. She's coming through tonight with Laura—my brother's daughter."

Pip looked him over again. "You seem different from the way you were at the fossmere, or on *Tulpenmanie*."

"Why—because I don't have a baby attached to my ear or a fig in my hand?"

"No—different. Less . . ." She let her voice trail off, unable to put the impression into clear words.

"Ah." Tane nodded in comprehension.

Pip saw he still wore his earring and the braided ring on his wedding finger, and a silver chain that vanished under his shirt. She thought it was the one that had charms representing Jillian Jules and their children. The rest of the clinking silver ornaments had presumably been left aside with his kilt.

He leaned forwards and closed the distance.

Mostly, anyone coming that close would send Pip into reverse unless she was working, but it was difficult to be stand-offish with Tane. He had breathed air into her lungs and jumped off a yacht with her in his arms in the prelude to the most glorious holiday she'd ever had, and which was still paying dividends.

Bless Lupin for giving me that voucher. I wish I could tell her what it means to me.

Thinking of lost opportunities, Pip resolved to make sure Jan and her daughter Clarkia, at least, knew how happy she was to have them back in her life.

Tane bent almost double and said, into her ear, "You think I'm different because I'm dialled down."

"What? Oh."

He stood back and gave her a solemn nod. "Love bubbles turned off. Linda says I have to do that when I go to a festival."

Linda, Pip recalled, was his sister-in-law . . . her young friend Jamie's mother. She'd never met Linda, but Tane seemed to love her, although probably not in a way to make his brother bristle. He was certainly in awe of her.

"Love bubbles," she said thoughtfully. "Sounds like something in a pink bottle."

"I know, but that's what Linda calls it."

He grinned at her, and suddenly the beautiful attraction he wielded at the fossmere and on *Tulpenmanie* returned. Pip was tempted to go in for a hug, but she stayed put. Generally she didn't hug, although she'd decided she would continue to make an exception for Jan and Clarkia, if they wanted.

"That," Tane said, grinning. He bent again and gave her an affectionate kiss on the brow.

"Yes, well, turn it off. If you keep that up, you'll frighten the nice boy at the T-shirt stall and get ravished by passing women."

"But not by you."

"Not by me."

Tane laughed. "Miss Pearmain, I like you a lot."

"So you said, before. I like you, but you're dangerous."

"Not to you, though."

"No. You're young enough to be my son, and you're married to someone you call your love twice over, and whom I like and respect. How's Jillian Jules?"

"My forever love is as beautiful as ever. Jane did say you'd been to dance with her a couple of times this week. Jill was sorry she missed seeing you. Jules was, too."

"I was pushed for time. The first time, I had an escort from a guesthouse, and the second time Ardal fetched me."

"Yes—and obviously Ardal got you safely back to the castle bridge gate? Unless you came via the Charm Lines and the cliff gate?"

"Ardal took me to the castle and Edgar fetched me through

in time for pick-up. And I even got to jump over some logs on Fimber. That's the pony Ardal lets me ride."

He nodded his understanding.

"They were both very helpful." She paused a beat and added with gentle malice, "Neither of them lost me between the fossmere and the gate."

Tane threw up one hand to acknowledge a hit. "I wouldn't have lost you either if you hadn't pulled loose. And I did send Jane to find you."

"So you did." Pip tilted her head up. "You said Jane will be here later — am I likely to run into anyone else from the fossmere?"

It would be lovely to see them, although she probably wouldn't have time to socialise once filming began.

"Not this time — oh, wait. Sam and Oash might come. It depends if Oash can manage the stress of being humanside . . ."

"I'll say hello if I see them."

Sam was Tane's stepdaughter, or daughter-by-love as the fay phrased it. She was partly human, but Oash, her friend, lover, or partner . . . Pip was unsure which . . . was a pureblood sylvan and as such she found the air and water on the human side of the gates difficult to handle.

Pip turned away, but Tane touched her arm. "What's this?"

Pip raised her wrist to show him. "It's a puppy charm someone gave me. Isn't it lovely?"

He ran his fingers over it. "And so it should be. My dad made this, and he's never made a bad piece in his life."

"Did he indeed?" The charm wasn't signed, but she didn't doubt him. Silversmithing ran in the family, and she had met his dad, Merryn Pendennis. "It was a present to me from someone called Gillan St Ives. Do you know her?"

Tane nodded. "Her man's a cross-cousin to Dad, and to me for that matter, but they live human mostly. I'll tell him you're wearing it. He'll be pleased. Do you know what that is?"

"A puppy charm," Pip said.

"Yes, that's the shape, but it's also something called a promise blank."

"A — oh, I see. Like a voucher?"

"A kind of come-to-me. It should attract someone . . . or something." He frowned, looking unusually uncertain. "If it's not what you want, you return the charm to the donor."

"Thanks for the explanation. I'll remember. I am supposed to wear it?"

He nodded. "That's right. It gets attuned to you that way. It won't do you any harm."

"I met your dad at a place called Smile o' the Glean. He was having a drink with the rest of Team Tam."

"Oh?"

"I quite saw why your mum picked him out to be your dad. He's lovely," she said.

Tane grinned and nodded. "Just as well, or I wouldn't be me."

"I suppose not. Anyway, say hello to your dad for me when you see him next," Pip said. She added, "Or is that greet you?"

"He understands either. He spends more time over here with you humans than I do. His lady and Linda's mam are best friends, and my sister Richenda and Linda's sister Ammie have been close since they were babies."

Pip cleared her throat. "Does his lady know about you?"

Tane laughed. "Of course she knows! Can you imagine my dad keeping that news from her . . . or even wanting to? She calls me *the son I love but didn't bear*. She and Mam are good friends, too, along with Eleanor Cliff — William's wife."

Pip knew William as another member of Team Tam, but she was pretty sure she hadn't met Eleanor. It was all somewhat tangled. She decided she'd had enough of unravelling pedigrees for one day, so she said goodbye to Tane and headed back to the T-shirt stall.

Jessie wasn't there, but Asher gave her a soft parcel which he said contained her shirt and the bonus dress.

Pip thanked him for his advice and made her way to the exit of the Icehouse.

She hadn't realised she was coming to a festival full of fairies.

Chapter Three. Whiskey for Magda

It took several wrong turns and a couple of encounters with acquisitive goats before Pip found her way to cabin six. She tried Goat-Morse, but the goats just tried to get their noses in her pockets. She was fending them off for a third time with verbal apologies, since they didn't seem to notice her Goat-Morse ones, when she heard a peremptory baritone bleat behind her.

Afraid she'd strayed into the path of a boss billy who might even now be revving up his horns to give her a shove, she turned to see a rotund grey-haired man who might have stepped out of a Bacchanalian painting. He jerked his head in an odd tossing gesture and bleated again. The goats turned their attention on him, and he fed them something dark and sticky from his shoulder bag. Pip recognised the smell from the treats Jane's friend Ardal gave the ponies.

"Gingerbread, despoinída," the man remarked unnecessarily. He might be Greek, Pip thought, remembering Theo Georgiou who used to own the Delmsford petrol station in the 1960s. Pip and her cousins had gone to school with his children, Vicky and Leto, who had sounded just like all the other kids at Delmsford State School. Maybe that was because their mum, Debs, was Australian. Theo had retained his native accent.

The man added, "I'll try to get them to stay away from the festival folk, but you know goats . . . At least, I expect so, since you didn't run away from them screaming."

"You're not Peter P are you?" Pip asked.

45

He laughed. "Lord, no! Why should I be?"

"Magda says he has goats."

"I don't have goats. They just like me." He pulled some pipes out of the leather bag.

"Panpipes?" Pip asked. She entirely understood his stance on ownership and goats. She didn't have cats. They just liked her. Sort of.

"Eight-reeds. You play the pipes?"

"No. I dance to them. To just about anything, really."

"Then I hope to see you dance in the dawn with the rest of the young ones. I'll be playing in the supergroup every morning and for anyone else who needs music for dance during the day." He raised the pipes to his lips and began a skipping, tripping melody that drew the goats to him like pins to a magnet.

Pip stared after him delight as he retreated, followed by a multi-hued flock. The not-so-pied piper. A goat ballet began to caper in her mind.

Maybe a ballet for children. That way lots of them could do little solos. Goats were so . . . She strove to come up with the right adjective and settled upon *agile*.

She stepped into cabin six to find Magda sipping whiskey from a heavy crystal tumbler.

"You're welcome to join me — no — that's right, you don't drink spirits."

"I'll make my own drink." Pip rummaged in her case for the canister of camomile tea she'd packed at home. It was part of a set that had belonged to Little Nanna Pearmain and the lid fitted properly . . .unlike some of the modern ones, she grumbled to herself.

While the kettle came to the boil, she said, "Magda, are there any humans here besides me?"

Magda sipped again. "I'm mostly human. Seven-eighths via Mum, but maybe a bit less from Francine's influence. A quarterling at the very most, and probably not that."

"But I've just met all sorts of people and they were all—" She shrugged. "Tane Pendennis is here, and I know what he is—a pisky water halfling with no human in him at all. He says his daughter Jane is coming, and maybe his stepdaughter Sam, who is part sylvan. There were two lovely young people in the Icehouse who gave me these—" She displayed the package containing her shirt and dress. "I'm sure they were something. They both had interesting ears and not a zit in sight. Not pisky though, because they weren't glinting and clinking, though the girl had a bracelet. Then I met a Greek man who pied-pipered the goats. Only I don't think he was exactly Greek."

"Probably a herdfee man, if he was influencing the goats," Magda said. "As to the others—everyone we met at *Diamond Spellman Studio* is human, as far as I know. Matin Campania is an elf man, but his wife Tamzin is human. Well, I think she is. I met her at a gallery in Adelaide a couple of years ago, but I don't know if she'll remember me. That scamp you were stirring up at the gate is a pisky. Mullion something?"

"Mullion St Ives," Pip supplied.

"Ah. As I said, I don't know him, but I think his great-grandfather, or some such relation used to help Mum out with legal things. Mars St Ives, he was called. The lad looks just like him, but less reliable.

"Anyway, I'd say there will be far more humans here than anything else. Don't worry about it. Any fay this side of the gateway will be living human, at least temporarily, so there shouldn't be any flying violins."

"What?"

Magda gestured with her glass. "Or oak tables."

"What?"

"Or vanishing teapots."

"I don't understand."

"Really? After spending a week with them *au natural* during your V-S Experience?"

"They wore clothes mostly, if by *them* you mean the family at the fossmere."

Magda gave an unladylike snort. "Clothes! Who cares for clothes? That's not what I meant."

"Then tell me what you did mean." Pip was a mistress of obfuscation, prevarication, and side-stepping, but she didn't always appreciate it when someone turned it on her.

Magda drained her glass and contemplated the faceted crystal. "Tork gave me this. See?" She pointed to a decoration on one of the flat planes. "This symbol is mistletoe. Nothing to do with druids or that — it means kiss. He said we'd both missed out on too many kisses by being alone for years, and since he knows I'm partial to a drop of Tom Cat Hill's finest, he gave me this to use when I'm away from him. It's a kiss from him, see. He still loves to kiss me. At *my* age."

Pip saw that kiss-from-a-glass might be romantic, or possibly creepy on some level, but she failed to understand what it had to do with Magda's cryptic remarks. She wondered how old Magda's husband was. Surely not over a hundred. Not many men made it to that age. Little Pop Pearmain was the only one of her lost family to live to be ninety, and he said he did it only because he'd promised Little Nanna he'd hold on to celebrate their seventieth wedding anniversary. Having done so, he lived on for almost another year because, as he put it, he'd got into the habit. He'd died . . . no, he'd gone to glory . . . peacefully while snoozing on their favourite seat in the garden.

Pip thought maybe she should revise her dancing centenarian ambition downwards. Even a dancing nonagenarian would be impressive, though ninety didn't have quite the cachet of a hundred. After all, more than four percent of her peers would make it that far.

She did wish Lupin had been able to be one of them.

Lupin had been so decided, and so full of energy. She'd had so much presence . . . why had she gone early when so many bored and boring people lingered on in a kind of a beige haze?

Maybe she crammed as much living into seventy years as most people manage in eighty.

Magda went on, "What I'm getting at is that fay — full fay, not catch and toss folk like me — have talents they don't choose to show off in public when visiting humanside. One of them is conjuring. With me so far?"

Pip snapped her mind back to the subject at hand and said, cautiously, "Rabbits out of hats?"

"They don't do that. They can't. They can't conjure any-thing . . . I want to say alive, but really, it seems to depend on sentience. Tork conjured a bunch of mistletoe down to use as a template for my glass. If he'd tried for a bird in the same tree, it wouldn't have worked. They also can't conjure money, or limousines, or anything they couldn't get by their own hon-est efforts otherwise. Your own ring you accidentally left in someone's barn? No trouble . . . as long as you can get a fix and know where you left it. A ring from a jeweller's case that you have no right to take? No. It seems to come down to in-tention, or possibly I mean a cultural tabu."

Something went ding in Pip's brain.

"Jin . . . Jisinia that is . . . got my phone out of my hand when I was on the yacht. She was nowhere near me. Was that conjuring?"

"Very likely," Magda said. "She shouldn't have done it. It's bad manners. In fact, she shouldn't have been able to . . . it's not an exact science."

"Zach made her give it back."

"Hmm. Very likely none of the fay here at the festival will be conjuring things about in public. Or, if they do, they'll be discreet about it."

"Why?" Pip asked.

Magda said, "Think about it."

"So as not to scare the humans?"

"Partly."

"That could be easily solved by just coming clean."

"Think some more."

Pip thought. "Oh."

"Now you're getting it." Magda poured herself another finger of whiskey from a bottle. The label showed a silhouetted cat perched on a hill. Presumably it came from a distillery near Magda's gallery.

Must tell Kittisack.

"You think it might cause trouble for them."

"Got it in one." Magda toasted her with the glass. "Fay have better health than humans. Even such a small a percentage of fay blood as I have means somewhat better health. It's unpredictable, though . . . my father died of Spanish flu, and technically he should have had more fay blood than me. Better health means good teeth, no allergies, good skin, fewer weight problems, strong bones, good digestion . . . that might come down to the luck of the draw. Among humans you get supermodels, and elite athletes—winners of the genetic lottery. You get fully human people who make their century and who never have a filling . . . or who smoke for seventy years and never get a bad cough. Again, luck of the genetic draw."

Pip said, "But?" She knew there was a but there somewhere.

"But—genetic lottery won't give a pure human or a tracer the ability to conjure. I can't do it." She shrugged. "There's enough envy around already on the human playing field. To have the full fay—and the halflings and even some quarterlings—out there flinging violins about would cause far too much ill-feeling, so generally, they don't."

"Can't see why," Pip objected. "As you say, there are huge

variations in what humans can do. For instance, I've been practising ballet every weekday for decades, but no amount of practice would make me into a principal dancer even if I was young enough. For one thing, I'm probably too small. For another, I just don't have whatever it takes. I might envy someone who has the talent and the stature I don't, but I wouldn't hold it against her."

Magda downed the whiskey. "Have you ever heard of the witch trials?"

"Salem?"

"And England. Scotland. Norway. Mind, I'm not saying the fay are witches—they're not, and never have been as far as I know. But they can do things others might perceive as magic, though they don't call it that. As I said, conjuring can't be used to do harm, but I bet that wouldn't stop the occasional idiot trying to weaponise it—or the fay who used it. Talk about a rock and a hard place! Picture a hapless elf man being forced to conjure arrows into someone's hide. He couldn't possibly do it. Into a bag of straw? No problem! Into a person? No way. And it wouldn't be bravery or moral stance holding him back. He literally could not do it. Try explaining that to some righteous bully or determined torturer! So—better not to flaunt the ability in public, and better not to mention one's bloodline unless or until someone asks directly."

Pip thought that courtesy might be applied to lots of things, such as political opinion, dietary habits and the state of one's toes.

Looking back, she realised she had seen conjuring at work. Not only had Jin got her phone, but at the fossmere Trae had sent a tea tray over . . . remarking to Jane that he'd try not to dump it on her head. Jillian's daughter Sam had asked her partner, Oash, to toss her a towel for Pip, but the toss had been far longer and more accurate than should have been possible even for an athletic young woman, which was the way Oash presented.

Pip was nearly sure she'd seen Mullion St Ives do it, quite apart from morphing into a black Scottie, when he'd suddenly had a pen to scribble a countersignature on her declaration. Ardal Cornfellow, Jane's hob friend, had produced gingerbread from somewhere for her to gift to the pony Fimber after he carried her smoothly over a jump.

Okay, so she had seen conjuring, but her mind had edited it out, just as it had tried to edit Mullion's sudden appearance after the altercation with the little dog at the Fairy Gardens.

"Hmph," she said.

"Quite so," Magda said, raising her glass to her lips and taking it away. Evidently, it was now empty, so maybe she was kissing her husband by proxy.

"Pity," Pip said. "I wouldn't have minded seeing a flying fiddle as long as it was nowhere near my head."

Magda glanced at her bottle, shook her head, went to the little sink, and replaced the bottle and rinsed glass in her case. "That had better be my lot. I have a slightly better tolerance for alcohol than my apparent peers, but if I drink too much I get maudlin."

Pip re-boiled the kettle and belatedly made her tea.

Over her shoulder, she said, "Speaking of apparent peers, how do you explain your age away to doctors? You must be over a hundred, but you sure don't look it."

"I rarely go near the creatures. If I have to present myself for any reason, I use glamoured documents that suggest I'm seventy or so. Tork sees to it for me . . . and before you ask, my driver's licence is legitimate and it's in my married name. The only glamouring is to let folk see what keeps them comfortable. Tork doesn't mind. I look about his age anyway. Before we married, I told him I was much older than him, but he didn't think it mattered. I used to think at least I'll never be left alone again . . . and, dammit, that was hubris, because it looks as if—" She passed a hand over her eyes, "I shouldn't have had that last refill. Told you whiskey makes me maudlin."

"What if someone finds out how long your gallery has been trading?" Pip asked. She chose not to pursue Magda's comment. Lupin's passing had shown her how little one could depend on remaining time.

"Been snooping, have you?"

"Not yet."

"Don't bother. The date's not on the website, and even if it was, people would assume it was opened by my mother or grandmother . . . or maybe a convenient aunt." She grinned suddenly. "Magda Quest? Oh, you mean the first Magda Quest? Magdalena . . . yes, it's a family name. We've been mixed up with the arts forever." She dropped the act. "It's even true. My mother was a Marianna, but her mother was a Magdalena. My own Marianna has sons, so the name question didn't come up . . . Maybe they'll spawn another Magda someday, but that's up to them and their kinder-makers. Besides, they're all Mackenzies."

Pip wrinkled her brow over that one and dredged up an answer from her perusal of The Orders of the Fay. "Mackenzie is a braeside name?" she ventured.

Magda clicked her tongue and flicked her fingers at Pip. "Got it in one. My son-by-love has pure heather blood running through him. He comes from a place called Heather Isle. He's what they call a red Mackenzie. Looks verra weel in the green tartan."

"I see," Pip said. She supposed that meant a namesake for Magda would more likely be a Morag or some such name. According to Edgar's books, some of the orders of the fay clung closely to traditional names. "What's his name?" she asked.

"Arran," Magda said. She spelled it out. "And the boys are

Banner, Tavish, and Tammas. Not an alpname among them."

Pip nodded and took her tea over to the bed Magda hadn't chosen. They were both the same anyway. She saw they could be pushed together to make a double if anyone chose. She didn't choose. She settled cross-legged on the bed with her tea and the second volume she'd borrowed from Edgar, resolved to do some solid study so she could go order-spotting the next day.

First, though, she took out her phone and called her cousin, Jan. There was no point in resolutions to do better by her remaining relatives if she didn't make an effort to stay in contact.

"Pip? Is everything okay?" Jan sounded worried.

"Everything is fine. I got the film part, and I'm at Delphinium Island, where we'll be shooting."

"What—are they scouting locations or something? Rehearsing? Have you met the stars?"

"No to all. We'll be doing the filming this week."

"That sounds—that isn't the way it usually works—is it?"

"Not at all, from my experience. It might be wonderful or a freaking disaster."

"You don't sound as if you care much."

"I don't. I'm having far too much fun. Anyway, I have my agent on-set. She'll take care of any little speedbumps." She widened her eyes at Magda, who widened hers right back.

She was obviously listening in.

"That's good," Jan said.

"Have you spoken to Clarkia today?" Pip asked.

"No—is everything—"

"Everything was fine when I called her yesterday. She's such a useful person."

"Um—well, I like her," Jan said cautiously.

"You should be very pleased with how she's turned out."
Okay, so that sounds weird.

Hurriedly, she switched the subject. "Jan, you remember

when we were talking about *Grandmother's Sunshine,* and you told me there was a photo of Callie and Cammie some- where?"

"Yes—but I don't know where it is. I just remember Little Nanna mentioning it. Why?"

"Do you know what Little Nanna Laurel's name was be- fore she married Little Pop?"

"Heavens, Pippin—you mean you don't?"

"I never asked. She was just Little Nanna Laurel, Anth to Little Pop or Missus Laurel to other people."

"I'm sure it's on the flyleaf of some of her books . . . but in any case, it was Bay."

"Bay as in horses? Or Bay as in Jellico Bay? Or—"

"Bay as in the bay tree, I assume. The bay laurel. That's how I remember her maiden name, because she used to say she might have changed the sound, but not the meaning."

"So she used to be Schizanthus Bay." Again, she caught Magda's eye, and repeated the name for her benefit. "Schizan- thus Bay."

"Right. Big Nanna was Hazel Petit . . . which is mad, since the name means small, and darling Big Nanna was anything but."

Pip waited, not wanting to ask for the last name, since Little Nanna Pearmain was no relation at all to Jan and Lupin—ex- cept by love—and so she should be the one to know it.

Jan added, "Your Nanna Pearmain was originally Picotee Beck. That name means a creek or a stream. Pippin, what is this all about?"

Pip sighed. "It's complicated." She considered the whole sprawling mass of things discovered, discussed, and pon- dered since she'd argued about tea with the airline staff on Wednesday evening. She'd have to make a big effort to sort it out. "I'll tell you all about it when I come home, Juniper Jam Tart. I promise I will. Just now, too much is happening."

"I'll hold you to it," Jan said. "But listen, Pip, if you want to play at family trees, get Clarkia to show you what she's done. She started one for school and got hooked on the hunt. I don't know how far she got, but she's bound to have kept it. There's no point in running over the same ground twice."

"Thanks! I will ask her — when I get back. Maybe you can come and have dinner or something? And stay the night? Then we can sort out who knows what and pool the information."

"I will, if you get in some more of those tarts," Jan said.

"There are always tarts. I've even found some new flavours to order. Adam and Eve, and Marigold Magic. How's your new book going?"

"Nearly finished. It's been a bit of a slog, with Lupin and all."

"Yes. I'm looking forward to reading it, after I get Garter-stakes, which is coming in the post. Jan, you do signed copies, don't you?"

"Yes, why? I can't imagine you want one? Obviously, I'll do it if you do."

"There's a woman called Gillan St Ives who offered to get me a puppy. She wants a signed book. Not a freebie. She'll buy it, then send it to you for signing."

Jan said, "A puppy? But what about your beautiful cats?"

Pip didn't remind Jan that the cats weren't hers. Instead she said vaguely, "It's an idea, that's all . . ."

"You seem to be having a great many ideas these days," Jan said, laughing. "I'd better go, Pippin — that hissing sound you hear is my soup splattering out from under the pan lid. Good luck with the filming."

She hung up, beating Pip to the punch.

But at least, thought Pip, she hadn't said *toodles* the way Frances le Fay did when Pip spoke to her about getting Xavier What's-his-name to make her a new bucket.

Toodles. Who says that?

Magda was staring at her. "A puppy? From someone connected with the St Ives family? Are you nuts?"

Pip opened the encyclopaedia and started to read about fijordfee. They sounded northern, stern, and full of fortitude.

Must be all that ice and snow.

Magda took the hint.

CHAPTER FOUR. DANCING IN THE DAWN

It was still dark when Pip heard the music.

She opened her eyes and hit the bedside lamp while she groped for her phone.

Volume two of Orders of the Fay, which was called Delftvolk, Elves, Fijordfee, and Fisherfolk, started to slide off the bed, and she grabbed it before it hit the floor.

Five o'clock. Really?

The music continued — a bright, sparkling air played on a violin.

More instruments joined in, one by one. She heard a drum, something with strings, a keyboard, and pipes.

It's the goatman's song.

Pip scrambled out of bed and into the tiny bathroom, where she splashed her face and tied up her hair in a rough bun. She snagged her parcel from the foot of her bed, pulled it open, and extracted the first garment to hand. It was the dress. She dropped it over her head, and it settled in a swirl of gathers to mid-calf. It would do.

Pip pulled on the soft slippers she mostly used for dancing and let herself out of cabin six.

She followed the music towards an open area, where soft light emanated from a circle of lamps.

More instruments joined in — Pip identified a harp and, with a catch of nostalgia, a lute.

Her mind flashed back to being sixteen, to performing as

Marigold Heriot in *The House of Heriot,* and to listening to
Alain Barfleur play his lute in the green room, just for her.

She looked about and found the lute-player. This one was
a young man in his twenties. He was playing it up for the
crowd and flirting with a pretty young woman holding a
horse.

A horse. Well, why not? There were goats, and Matin had
mentioned a horse and a pony. Maybe the woman was his
wife. If so, what did he think of having a handsome young
rooster luting at her?

The violinist, standing on a raised dais, had wavy brown
hair spilling over the shoulder of a green dress. Pip saw let-
tering across the chest and squinted to make it out.

Tamzin Campania — *Arts in Tune.*

Ah, not the woman with the horse then. This was Matin's
wife — the woman Magda had met at an art show, and who
was both musician and artist.

Pip looked at her with respect and avarice. This was the
woman she wanted to grill about music for her ballet, and
whose Magic Fiddle album she wanted to obtain.

The violin sang and laughed, playing phrases to which the
other instruments responded.

The goatman from yesterday was there, playing his pipes
and surrounded by entranced goats. Across from him, an
older woman sat at something that looked like a piano gone
wrong. Pip thought it might be a clavichord or a spinet. Its
sharp tone blended with the gentle notes of his pipes. Her
shirt said Mim Capricorn, *Supergroup.*

The piece ended and the violinist shifted into a waltz tune,
Silk and Circumstance.

Pip's feet moved automatically into the opening steps of
her ballet. As she danced, a swarm of dancers rushed past her,
parting like a river around a small rock. She knew they were
dancers because they moved that way.

Some of them bent and stretched, while others leaped into

an instant pattern of free dancing. There seemed to be no particular steps. Pip let the excitement carry her along.

The woman with the horse spun in a circle, with her preposterously wide dress flowing about her. A very young couple, dark-haired and shining, began a pas de deux, mirrored by a plus-sized woman in a sunset-coloured gown and a gigantic Scotsman in a kilt.

Braesider! Pip was pleased to identify another order of the fay. He had red hair, which was apparently common to the order. She wasn't sure about the woman, who had dark hair and a satisfied expression.

Pip found she was laughing. She'd never known anything like this. A girl in a white dress decorated with lemon daisies performed some careful pliés, working earnestly alongside a tall woman with straight brown hair that gleamed like a conker.

Something caught at Pip's recognition centre, and she danced through the crowd for a closer look.

"Jane!"

Jane's face lit in a beatific smile, and she flung herself at Pip.

"Miss Pip! What are you doing here?"

"Dancing," Pip said.

Jane turned to pull her companion forward. "Miss Pip, this is Laura. Laura, Miss Pippin Pearmain is the one making the dolphin ballet." She clasped her hands in her ecstatic fashion. "Miss Pippin, I had a wonderful idea about your ballet. I found you a principal to dance the Delphine role. Come and see . . ." She grasped Pip's hand and tugged her through the crowd. "Look!"

Pip looked obediently at the dancer Jane indicated. She saw — Delphine.

The dancer had a shock of thick fair hair, and her simple white dress was almost hidden under a mass of twinkling silver brooches and chains. She danced with fine technique, but also with joyful abandon, as if her mind was somewhere else and her body simply responded to the music.

"Oh!" Pip found herself clasping her hands in an unconscious parody of Jane.

She stepped forward to intercept the dancer. She was never going to let this one get away.

The music changed again to a fast-paced whirl.

A group of men, ranging from twenty-somethings to boisterous seventy-pluses, whooped and joined crooked elbows to dance in a row, pointing their toes and stepping with neat precision.

Dad Ballet, I assume!

Pip looked at their happy faces.

Jane raised her arms and began a step dance. "Come on, Miss Pippin—it's easy!"

It wasn't ballet. Pip had no idea what it was, but she saw the violinist dancing the steps on her dais, smiling with evident delight.

The young dark couple shouted and bounced into action, and the silver dancer followed. She turned, seeming to look for someone.

"You! Here! Now!" she shouted in a voice Pip heard clearly over the music.

An olive-skinned man who was possibly thirty or so made a *who—me?* gesture, and the silver girl beckoned imperiously.

They danced together, as if they were alone.

Pip judged him not as good as his partner, but that was more about her talent than any lack of his. He was good-looking, with that odd skin tone, and big—and strong.

All right. She'd found her seafay man.

And those men could be fiddler crabs . . . She gave them a sly, acquisitive glance. *I have plans for you.*

Pip relaxed and let herself respond to the music.

The lanterns faded as the sun rose, and everyone broke into

spontaneous applause.

The violinist raised her fiddle over her head. "Thank you everyone, and welcome to *Dance in Tune!* Thank you for dancing in the dawn. I'll see you all tomorrow at five o'clock."

She turned to descend from the dais, and Pip saw Matin Campania waiting for her. He had a little girl in his arms.

Jane seemed to be tying herself in knots with excitement, and Pip put a hand on her arm to ground her.

"Oh, Miss Pippin, wasn't it glorious! I love, love, love that music."

"So did I," Pip said. "Do you know what any of the pieces were called? Apart from *Silk and Circumstance*, I mean."

"The first one was *Chorós Capricornus*. That means dance of the goats. It's a herdfee tune. Isn't it fun? I didn't know all the others . . . they were all waltzes, but that last one was *Grá Damhsa*—dancing love. It's my absolute favourite tune, ever. The leprechauns play it at weddings or cruthú teaghlaigh. That's *make a family*, which is what some leppys do instead of weddings."

Pip could see why they might choose such a joyful tune.

The dancers and musicians were dispersing, probably getting ready for breakfast or whatever else was on their morning agenda. The men of *Dad Ballet* trooped by with towels around their necks as if they'd just been to the gym.

Pip smelled cooking and coffee, and noted the Icehouse was already awash with activity.

She realised Jane was staring at her dress with an odd expression.

She hoped she hadn't danced herself into a wardrobe malfunction, but when she looked down, she saw the pretty green and pink dress Asher Castleby had pressed upon her was decently arrayed. "What's wrong?" she asked.

Jane said, "I knew you were in films, but I didn't know you were actually a film star."

"I'm not. How do you know about film stars, anyway?"

"Laura and Jamie showed me some lovely films with people dancing when I went to see them last. The called them classic musicals. My favourites have Leona Irene and Victor Albert in them. They were *so* good."

Jane pulled out a panel of the dress and Pip saw the embroidery Jessie must have put on it—a large pink and green star. The familiar *Arts in Tune* was there, but above it she'd put *Film Star*.

"Oh, for—" Pip wanted to storm off and give Jessie a good bollocking, but she remembered in time that she'd signed a declaration of no harm, so she contained herself. "It's someone's idea of a joke," she said.

Jane smiled. "It's lovely. And look, it's really a button-on patch, so you can take it off later."

"I suppose so. But Jane, who were all those dancers? Not the men . . . I know they must be *Dad Ballet,* but the others. And why did you tell your cousin about my ballet?"

Jane said, guilelessly, "It's such a lovely idea, so of course I told Laura. I showed her the choreography we did, and she says it's really good, because the dolphin entry can be danced by people without much experience but developed more for professionals. I couldn't show her the principal roles, because I'm not remotely good enough to do them justice, but I told her about the story, and she said the *Forevers* might put it on. That's the dance troupe I'm hoping to join one day. What do you think? They just finished up performing at the Counterpoint Festival last week, and they've been looking for something new to add to their repertoire."

Pip wrestled with a weird mix of emotions. She had shared the development of *Delphine* with Jane, and she hadn't sworn her to secrecy. Why would she? Jane was a fairy girl living at the fossmere, so who would she tell?

Cousin Laura, apparently! From what Pip had gathered,

Cousin Laura was a halfling, but she'd always lived in the human world. Cousin Laura would have a driver's licence, and send emails, and talk in coffee queues or round the water cooler and go clubbing.

Having Cousin Laura know was a long way from playing at choreography with impressionable Jane.

Yes, she'd loved sharing it with Jane, but *Delphine* was her own project and not to be shared elsewhere until or unless she chose.

You didn't tell Jane that.

I shouldn't have had to!

She teetered on the edge of saying something sharp to Jane but overcame the urge. What harm could it do for the girl to daydream?

Pip had had no proper plans for *Delphine* beyond going to the Jellico Bay school and asking if they'd let her get up a little ballet with the children.

She didn't think Jane could arrange for an actual ballet troupe to work with her — but they were at the festival and honestly, what harm could it do?

You can get snubbed – the way Alison Blake snubbed you over Grandmother's Sunshine.

Ja? Und?

And — just possibly Jane *could* do this. She remembered Jules telling her Jane was extremely self-willed and stubborn when he and Tane took her out to Hob's Island at the end of her V-S Experience. If Jane set her mind to anything, Jules implied, that thing would happen. Conversely, if Jane decided no, then that thing would not happen.

Pip hoped nice Ardal Cornfellow would not be too shattered in his soul if Jane decided no, Ardal and Jane were not going to happen. He'd told her that apart from a few ventures to a pub called *The Harvest Hob*, he didn't go humanside. It was evident that Jane did. She apparently visited her cousins quite often, and she was planning to stay with her Brisbane-based grandmother for a time, and also to dance with the *Forevers*.

Pip gave a mental shrug. It was nothing to do with her. If Ardal wanted Jane in a romantic capacity, in the short term or for always, he'd have to either overcome his unease about the human realm or else offer Jane something she'd want more than her plans and ambitions.

She said, as evenly as she could, "Do you really think dancers that good would want to deal with me and my little ballet? That girl in the silver—"

"That's Richie," Jane said.

"Richie what? And is she a pisky?"

"Richenda Pendennis. She's my aunt. Sort of. She's a halfling, but she threw hard to the pisky side." She appeared to reflect. "You know Dadda has a semi-brother . . . from Grandad Pendennis."

"Yes. He's Jamie's dad, right? The one married to Linda."

"That's it. Uncle Jory. Dadda has a semi-sister too . . . only she's Uncle Jory's whole sister. She and Laura and Ammie Trip, who is lovely and not much bigger than you are, have been best friends forever as well as being one another's aunts and nieces and things. They all dance, but Richie is the only one who has principal solo talent. Anyway, Richie would love to dance Delphine."

"But why?" Pip asked. She remembered Tan mentioning a sister called Richenda and slotted the pieces together.

Jane gave her a sweet smile, with just a hint of steel behind it. "Darling Miss Pippin, she'll love to do it because I asked her."

Pip nodded gravely. "I see. Do you think *Dad Ballet* would like to join in?"

"Is that those men?"

"Yes. I thought—fiddler crabs."

"Oh!" Jane laughed and clapped her hands with apparent

delight. "Of course fiddler crabs! They can dance on the sand with Delphine."

She sketched some precise sideways steps with her arms at odd angles.

"Exactly." Pip grinned. Jane might not be principal material, but she had something that was even better, from Pip's point of view.

She got it.

Chapter Five. The Amphora Horn

After her initial announcement, Jane went on to assure Pip that Richenda's man, Corin, would be equally delighted to dance the seafay man. Not because Jane asked him, but because Richenda would want it.

"She trusts him to catch her, you see. He'll do anything for Richie. He's loved her for so, so long, but he's ten years older so he thought it wouldn't be suitable."

"And now he thinks it is?"

Jane laughed. "No, he doesn't think so, but he knows so. That's why they're betrothed."

She seemed to think that explained it.

Pip was tempted to strike while the iron was hot, but while she'd been talking to Jane, the dancers and musicians had all dispersed.

Fortunately, there was plenty more festival left . . .

Jane said, brightly, "Miss Pip, will you join me for practice?"

"Didn't we just do it?"

"No! That was Dancing in the Dawn. It was special. We need to practise our technique. If I'm going to dance with the *Forevers* next year or the year after, I have to get good enough. Laura says they won't take just anyone, even if they are related to Richie."

"Do you know what time it is?" Pip asked.

"About half-past-six if you mean clock time."

"That gives me time for a cup of tea. I'll meet you back here at seven. Will someone play for us, or shall I bring my phone?" She'd never used her phone while dancing with Jane because phones didn't work at the fossmere.

"Master Capricorn said he will play for us, if we don't mind dancing around the goats."

The return to routine suited Pip well. As she ran through basic exercises using a barre someone had set up, she let her mind dwell on the hopes of hot water and lemon at eight. She hadn't brought lemons to the festival, but she was sure someone would provide them.

After half an hour of diligent and calming exercises, Jane suggested dancing something from *Delphine*.

Pip complied, first asking Master Capricorn, as Jane referred to their piper, if he had any music that would work for dolphins playing porthole tag.

"Let's see now . . . give me the tempo."

Pip and Jane danced some steps, and the piper nodded. "The eight-reed's not the best for what you want. My other main instrument's the lyre, but an amphora horn would work for this."

"What's that?" Pip asked when Jane didn't.

The piper said, "An old instrument from my part of the world."

"Can you show us?"

He looked startled. "I didn't bring one with me."

"You can get one though. Conjure it?" Pip urged.

Capricorn dropped his gaze.

"Call the goats round, then no one will notice."

He looked up with dark eyes filled with mirth. "For you, despoinída—"

He took some gingerbread out of his bag and the goats, which never seemed far from him, crowded in.

When he'd finished distributing the sticky treat, he dusted his hands together as if to clean them. After that, he lifted an odd-looking item into view.

Pip saw at once why it was called amphora, but horn?

It seemed to be made of pottery, beautifully decorated with dolphins.

"This belonged to my patéra," he said. "To hear him play would draw the dolphins from the deeps. I'm not the man he was, but I'll try. Give me the sequence again."

The music that came from the amphora horn was eerie, as if playing underwater, but it carried a tune and a surprisingly varied tone.

Pip and Jane tried the sequence, and, after the first strangeness, the music felt right.

After a while, the sound was augmented by two young men playing a sweet-toned flute and a weird-looking drum with strings. Pip had no idea what that was. She turned to look and saw four more dancers had joined them — the young dark couple, a woman possibly in her forties, and a man of around the same age wearing a shirt that proclaimed him as Grant Chapman, of *Dad Ballet*.

With six dancers, the sequence took shape, as they followed one another in and out of imaginary portholes.

They came to the part where Delphine should enter, and Pip called a halt.

The players stopped, and someone applauded from the side.

"Lovely bit of improv." It was the silver dancer.

"Richie!" Jane went to hug her.

"Hey, Janie. Is this the piece Laura was talking about? And is there any more of it?"

Jane indicated Pip. "It's Miss Pippin's ballet. She has the choreography written down, but we haven't got music yet."

"That will do nicely for this part," the girl said. She turned to Capricorn. "Is that a trad tune, master?"

"It was improvisation, as you suggested," he said.

"Can you do it again? And write it down?"

"I don't write music down," he protested.

"I do." A small dapper gentleman of indeterminate age and quiffed grey hair stepped forward. He had on a three-piece suit with a pale grey waistcoat, highly polished boots and a tuning fork. A gold tie-pin gleamed in the folds of a blue cravat. "Has anyone got some paper? No—never mind." He took a black object out of his deep pocket. "This'll do." He held a button down and the thing lit up with a row of red lights which slowly turned amber then green.

"Hit it," the gentleman said, holding up three fingers.

The musicians must have been as mesmerised as Pip felt, because they began the sequence again.

Pip came to her senses and started dancing, with Jane close behind. The other four joined in, along with Jane's cousin Laura and two more girls who must have been attracted by the music.

When they finished, the gentleman clicked his instrument off and beamed at them. "Got it. I'll transcribe it today. To whom shall I give the finished score? And do you want it in more than one key? I've never had experience with these particular instruments."

"What do you play?" asked the male half of the young couple.

"Bless you, not a thing, unless you count this." The gentleman held up the tuning fork. "I sing a capella with the Odd Gentlemen. I know music theory and notation, however." He nodded a greeting to Capricorn. "Someone said you were Costas Capricorn. Is that right?"

"It is."

"Grand. I hope Mim is well? Damned shame. Damned shame about Robert. This was his—he set us singing with this for thirty years."

Capricorn said Mim was well, and that she'd be playing her spinet later.

"Give her my love." The dapper gentleman beamed and took himself off.

Pip said, "Who the devil was that?"

No one seemed to know, but Capricorn said he'd ask Mim. "If he's sending her love, she ought to know his name."

It was eight o'clock by then, and Pip had a date with a lemon. She went in search of one.

Magda was drinking coffee in cabin six when Pip returned, carrying a basket of lemons, a bowl of strawberries and cream, and a dozen assorted tarts.

"You've had a productive morning," Magda commented.

Pip beamed at her as she unpacked her bounty. "You have no idea. I have the *Forever* troupe interested in workshopping *Delphine*, that nice herdfee man has composed some music for porthole tag, a little quiffy man with a tuning fork is writing our musical notation and I don't have to miss out on my strawberries and cream."

Magda said, "You're right about me having no idea. I have no idea what you're talking about."

Pip squeezed a lemon into a cup of water, drank it, sat down on her bed, and plunged a spoon into her strawberries. She supposed she should explain things to Magda, but she felt in need of a bit of silence. "I'll tell you later."

Magda said, "I hope you don't plan to wander off again, because you have a sound stage call for nine o'clock." She added, testily, "I trust you didn't forget why we're here?"

"Of course not," Pip said mendaciously. She ate her strawberries in record time, then began on the tarts. She felt as if she'd lived through a day already, and it was only half past eight.

Chapter Six. Sound Stage

Pip did not expect a horse to attend the sound stage call, but one was present. It was the grey that she'd seen at Dancing in the Dawn that morning. It stood to one side of the sound stage with the young woman sitting side-saddle and the handsome lutist leaning against a flat and holding a rein.

Jasper Diamond and Steward Bellaine the cameraman were there, along with a couple of others Pip remembered from the *Diamond Spellman Studio*. There was also a small crowd of people who were presumably actors, and probably a rep company, because they were chatting comfortably as if they all knew one another. She didn't recognise anyone, but then, she didn't expect to. It was a long time since she'd been in the film game, and longer still since she'd been on stage. Even then she'd never belonged to a company, although she'd been attached to some for various projects.

The sound stage looked thoroughly professional to her, and it must have had impressive acoustics and soundproofing, because the noise of the festival was nowhere. One side was open, allowing fresh autumn air to ruffle the horse's mane.

Pip stood near the entrance with Magda, waiting for something to happen. It wasn't unusual to be called for nine o'clock then spend the whole day waiting, only to be told to come back tomorrow when the same thing sometimes happened all over again. Pip had brought *Delftvolk, Elves, Fijordfee and Fisherfolk* along with her, as well as her messenger bag and a flask of tea.

She didn't think she'd see any delftvolk, fijordfee or fisher-folk at the festival, but she had high hopes of elves, since she'd already sighted at least three. Jessie and Asher from the T-shirt stall were two of them.

The third one, Matin Campania, was approaching now with a small dapper gentleman.

"That's my tuning fork quiffy man," she stage-whispered to Magda.

Jasper Diamond, looking a bit exasperated, turned to the newcomers with relief. "Matin — Humphrey — good to see you."

Humphrey?

Pip felt boggle-eyed. Tuning fork quiffy man must be Humphrey Carpenter-Rivers, the author of the script. He'd asked for her especially, so why hadn't he recognised her when she was dancing?

The men shook hands, then Diamond said, "Humph, what's with the horse?"

Humph — Pip thought she might as well accord him that name — beamed. "Jasper, right? Prologue."

"Since when is there a prologue? I've been all over the shooting script and there is no prologue."

"Since I saw this magnificent beast and his equally impressive master this morning and hatched one."

Diamond said, "All right — as there's nothing in the shooting script, you'll have to explain."

Humph got up on the stage, which was already set up as a hospital room with chairs, medical equipment and an apparent window. "In the original script, we never know what put Perdita in the coma. As soon as I saw this beast, I knew exactly what happened." He paused impressively. "Runaway brides make wonderful motifs, all flying veils and puffy meringue frocks. So — Perdita has married Stevo in a suburban sixties service and she's heading for a suburban sixties reception replete with bad jokes and rude telegrams about bedsprings. In the hiatus, the bridal party go off for photographs — with me so far?"

No one reacted, but he went on. "Stevo and his mates stop off for a slash, or a beer or something, and Perdita arrives in the park alone for the photo ops. Her bridesmaids have gone off to get a coffee . . . or to make repairs to a frock, or something. She's waiting all alone when Mister Handsome here rides up on his steed." He indicated the lutist, who raised a lazily amused eyebrow. "He offers her a quick spin on the steed, and she accepts —"

"Why would she do that?" Stew the cameraman asked, looking up from his light board. He sounded genuinely curious.

"Because what else has she to look forward to? Life as a sixties suburban housewife," one of the women said in an attractively husky voice. "Of course she's going to jump at the chance to go for a ride with a charming stranger. I would, in her shoes."

"Got it in one — who are you again?" Humph asked.

"Star," the woman said.

Pip saw with surprise that she was the forty-something dancer who'd joined in with her impromptu rehearsal.

"Are you sure you are?" Humph looked baffled.

"Star Calder-Quince. She's your Perdita, remember?" Jasper said.

"Oh, right, great." Humph turned to the woman. "I didn't recognise you dressed in that get-up. Have you done something to your hair? It looks different."

The woman, slim and grey-eyed with soft flyaway hair, gave an exaggerated sigh. "I usually have it tied up."

"Grand," Humph said. "Pin your brooch on your collar so I can fix on that."

The woman opened her small shoulder bag and pulled out

what Pip assumed was a brooch. She pinned it to her collar. "Okay?"

"Grand," Humph repeated. "So, Star, as Perdita, you get swept away on the horse by Jack the lad here and it's all soft-focus and romantic, and throbbing with lust with the wedding gown poofing about, only—Stevo and co show up, half cut, blowing their horns, spook the horse, up goes the horse, down goes the bride and—" He broke off, making an expressive gesture.

"That cannot be done on a sound stage," Jasper said. He sounded weary and patient.

"No need. It's a prologue, see? It's done in a green setting and projected onto a screen at the back of the stage. No lines. All over in five. Cut when they're all crowding around the fallen bride."

"And what do I do when I've allowed someone else's bride to fall off my steed?" the lutist asked.

"Court never would do that," the girl on the horse said decidedly.

"No, sweetheart, I never would in real life, but this would be acting."

Humph waved his hand, dismissing this. "I suspect you'd scarper, with big regret, leaving the rest of the party to find Perdita unconscious in the grass. You might even poof out of existence. So . . . you're a phantom of lost chances." He rocked forward on his toes and bounced. "Can you poof?"

"He can in post-production," Stew said.

"Grand. However you vanish, no one knows exactly what happened. We'll add a line to the first scene where Stevo says they'll ask Perdita for an explanation when she wakes up." He beamed at them all. "How's that, then?"

Jasper Diamond ran a hand through his greying hair. "Quite apart from the fact that this is the first I've heard of this—how do you expect us to fit it in? It needs a location . . .

not to speak of costume, and public liability, and rehearsal —
"

Humph said, "Don't you folk at *Diamond Spellman* pride yourselves on thinking on your feet? Isn't flexibility how you made your reputation back in the nineties? Isn't that why I picked you to bring my opus whatemy to the screen?"

"Yes, but —"

Matin Campania said softly, "You can use the greensward near the orchard, Jasper. If you don't have access to a wedding dress costume, we can provide one — we have designers and dressmakers here onsite. The liability issue shouldn't be a problem —" He turned to the lutist. "Court, your paperwork's up to date, I trust?"

"Yes, and I have all the performers' licences I need. So does Tansy." He indicated the girl on the horse and straightened away from the flat. "I take it you want Tansy to do the fall scene rather than your star?" He smiled at the woman cast as Perdita.

"I've done a bit of stunt-work but falling off a rearing horse is a bit more than I bargained for. I'm not sure you'd be covered if I broke something," the woman said.

The lutist shifted his attention to his — whatever she was. "Sweetheart?"

"I can do that," she said. "Mind, I'll want some padding on the arse, and make sure tha' drop me gently."

"I expect the costume could be padded. We'll dispense with a saddle, so you can slither off artistically rather than getting tossed to the four winds."

Humph looked ready to argue in favour of tossing the young woman to the four winds for theatrical effect, but Diamond shut him down. "You do anything you can do to make this safe," he said. "You are?"

"Court and Tansy Leopold, and the horse is Art." The lutist bowed. "I'm one half of the duo called Courtesan. My singing partner is off somewhere with her husband and son and Tansy's and my daughter."

"Else tha'd not hear tha'self think," his wife put in. "Right good lungs has our Cathie." She sounded proud of the fact.

Hob, Pip thought with secret glee. She recognised the tone and the accent from meeting Jane's friend Ardal and William Croft, who was part of Team Tam.

I'm so going to start a list of my fay-spottings.

"That's settled, then." Humph beamed at the assembled company. "Missus Leopold here is a bit big in the hips for Perdita, but since she'll be puffed out in a wedding meringue it won't matter."

"Did tha' just say I have a big arse, master?" Tansy enquired. She didn't sound angry.

Humph ignored that, and addressed the company as if he'd just walked in. "Hello, all. My name is Humphrey Carpenter-Rivers, but you may address me as Humph, or Your Highness. Take your pick. I wrote *Half-Life of the Lost* in the nineties but for one reason or another it was never performed. Now we're not only staging it but filming it and making a documentary of the making of. Busy-busy-busy, but who wants to be bored?" He turned to the cameraman. "You get that, lensman, or do you want us to do it again? I've got the audio." He showed off the black box he'd used earlier to record the dolphin music. "Okay—hit it again . . . action!" He resumed his spiel. "Since we're all in such a rush, I'll give you the cliff notes.

"Most of the cast come from Biblio-Rep, so you all know one another already. Hiring you as a job-lot saved weeks of auditions and screen tests because we know you all have chemistry together. The music is being supplied by *Arts in Tune*, under the auspices of Matin here, who is also providing the set, accommodation, food and entertainment. Our three new cast-members are Court and Tansy Leopold and—Art was it? They'll probably have just the one scene, but they'll be credited alongside the rest of you. We have one final cast member right here, and a highly important one. I don't know how many of you remember Tiny Pippin Pearmain, but she brings a long, long career of playing characters no one else would touch with a bargepole. Miss Pearmain will be filling the role of Solace, who is Perdita's consciousness. Please note Solace has no scripted actions or words. Her performance will be adlib. I have, however, marked her scenes in the scripts. When you see *Solace*, be ready to leave room for her input. When she's finished —"

Pip said, "You'll know when I finish. I'll fold."

A disconcerted silence ensued.

"I beg your pardon?" The woman playing Perdita smiled hopefully.

Pip hesitated. She knew what she meant. It was what she and Sully had dubbed the moment when she turned in on herself, disengaging with the audience or the camera. It was, she realised, something the same as when Tane Pendennis dialled down. She glanced at Magda, who shrugged.

"Fold," she said.

She mounted the steps to stand next to Humph. He wasn't a lot taller than she was, which was an odd sensation. Once, with Little Dad and Little Pops Pearmain and Laurel, she'd been used to compact males. Since Little Dad went to glory to pave the way for Little Mum, she'd barely met any adult man who didn't require her to tilt her head uncomfortably to meet his gaze.

"Give me a cue," she said to Humph.

He picked up a line that was probably Perdita's husband's from the script. "Perdy, you look lovely today. I've brought you some pink roses — your favourites. I'll call a nurse to put them in a vase."

He glanced aside and answered himself in a softer voice.

"I'll take those, Mister Stevens."

"Thanks, sister." He handed them over in mime, then became the nurse and arranged the roses.

"How is she really, sister?"

"As comfortable as can be expected . . ."

Exit nurse.

"Well, I'm going to find that damned doctor . . . when he comes back from his lunch. I'll see if I can get a straight answer from him."

He sighed and fussed with the flowers.

Pip stalked over and sniffed the invisible roses. "Typical! Stevo, where did you get the idea I was a pink roses person? I had white roses for my bouquet — didn't that tell you anything? Hello? White rose person here, with no babies' breath or fern flummery! Or maybe — firebird tulips! But you'd never give me those . . ." She held the pose for a couple of seconds then withdrew into herself and retreated to the corner of the stage. "That's folding," she said.

CHAPTER SEVEN. THE FIRST BRIDE

Pip went to watch the prologue scene being shot. Biblio-rep solved the wedding gown issue by opening up their costume hampers.

"We have everything from vampire cloaks to green pyjamas to asses' heads to trilbies," their wardrobe master said. "Bound to have a wedding dress or three somewhere."

His name was Ward, apparently, or that might have been just short for Wardrobe. He was middle-aged and flamboyant in a Rembrandt hat, and he called everyone darling.

Pip, watching him narrowly, decided it was a role he was playing, probably for his own amusement. He couldn't really be such a cliché.

Ward had evidently liaised with Aberdeen Diamond from *Diamond Spellman* over the costumes, because he had an enormous hamper—more of a skip—filled with street clothes ranging from the nineteen fifties up to contemporary pieces.

He also had a checklist on a giant whiteboard which listed character names, scene numbers, and costume codes.

Pip noted an interesting rate of attrition. Oz and Stevo, Perdita's brother and husband, had the most appearances, while Perdita's mother's visits stopped halfway through. Others began partway, as children gradually took over the ritual of visiting Aunt Perdie.

What about me? she wondered. She'd be onstage the whole time, along with the comatose Perdita. She'd been told she'd be wearing street clothes from the relevant time periods, but Ward, seeing her watching, beckoned her with a coy finger.

"Over here, darling."

Pip didn't like being beckoned, or called darling by a strange man, but Magda gave her a brisk tap on the arm.

"You said you weren't temperamental," she reminded.

Pip moved forward.

"Yes, you. Darling, I was told about you." Ward beamed at her like a child with a Christmas present. "You're a delight. I've decided you will wear these." He delved in the hamper and pulled out a pair of bib and brace overalls in dark blue. "I have applique patches to pin on to show the passing of time, and a selection of shirts in bright colours. There are also some outrageous costumes for the early years, but they add to the basics."

Pip had been told street clothes, keeping up with the times, but she saw how this would work.

"Bib and brace overalls have been around since the fifties . . . or before."

"Exactly, darling. The basic shape hasn't changed much, although the material is easier to wear now. Your appliques and shirts will colour-coordinate with the scene palette for each set. Do you do hats?"

Pip agreed that she did hats. It seemed a better option than a wig. She'd been wondering how they'd get around the hair . . . although . . . She looked over at Star Calder-Quince, whose hair was ash blonde and so not a million miles from Pip's no-colour flyaway locks.

Lupin's hair had turned iron grey and she'd worn it in a severe Eton crop. Jan's was thick and wiry, pepper-and-salt. Clarkia . . . Pip tried to picture Jan's daughter. Faintly ginger, she thought, although Clarkia might not appreciate the description. Anyway, hair colour these days was a matter of choice. If Clarkia didn't want to be faintly ginger, she might easily dye it brown. Or red. Or purple.

She nearly jumped out of her skin when Ward dropped a

boater on her head. "Crikey Daniel!"

Ward stood back and assessed the look. "Tres chic, mademoiselle."

Pip fixed him with a Look. "Ja. *Und*?"

Ward goggled at her and laughed. "Entschuldigung! Darling, I like you."

Pip wasn't sure she could return the compliment.

Star Calder-Quince applauded silently.

Ward, having apparently finished terrorising Pip for the moment, opened another skip and pulled out a folded garment bag.

"Wedding dress," he said. He turned his attention to Tansy Leopold, who remained perched on her horse. "Will you try this, darling?"

Tansy seemed about to say something, but her husband broke in, "She'll put it on all right. The only problem might be getting it off her!"

Tansy slid from the horse and for the first time Pip appreciated the sheer volume of cloth in her dress. It was made of cream calico, and it was smocked and tucked, falling in a mass of material to her calves. "Will it go over t'smock?" she asked.

"If you like—that might be best for padding, since you have to fall off the horse." Ward unsleeved the wedding dress from its protective cover. It was made of champagne silk, bouffant, and it had long, full sleeves. "There's a pillbox and veil, but maybe—"

Tansy advanced on him, took possession of the dress and turned it about. She pulled the zipper down, stepped into the dress, and settled it with a sinuous wriggle. "Do it up for me," she commanded, sliding into the sleeves.

Ward coaxed the zipper up, and went to adjust the garment, which was bunching around her.

Tansy fixed him with a firm gaze. "No." She bent, grasped the hem of her smock dress and tugged. With another wriggle, the bulges vanished. She got hold of the pillbox hat. "No hat," she decided.

"Okay, darling, we can go with a wreath of orange blossom."

Ward opened a hatbox and pulled out a slither of bags. He sorted briskly through them and came up with one containing a circlet of silk flowers. "This."

Tansy draped the veil and fixed it into place with clips he handed her. She had masses of soft brown hair which flowed under the veil.

"I don't think you could carry off a backcombed style to be in period. There's just too much of it," Ward said.

Humph, who had been rocking back and forth on his toes and beaming, said, "Long hair is the go. Long and free, because that's the real Perdita, under the conventional trappings. That's the Perdita who goes for it with the horse man."

Tansy turned to look down at Humph. "Court is a horse lord," she stated.

Humph beamed. "Then that's how we'll bill him in the credits. You can be the first bride, darling. Now what does he wear?" He turned to Ward, who was flourishing silk stockings and silver shoes at Tansy.

Pip rolled her eyes. These two showed signs of becoming a double act. Maybe they already were, as Humph seemed acquainted with at least some of Biblio-Rep.

"It depends on whether you see him as a real sixties horse rider, or a jockey riding exercise, or whether he's some kind of fantasy figure," he said. "Could go full on D'Artagnan."

"Does that imply he's in a pageant or a film?" Jasper Diamond asked.

Pip had the feeling he was out of his depth and was not accustomed to it and therefore resented it.

Humph wheeled to face him. "That's a thought—but no. I think we need not go into the horse lord's back story. He just *is*. He's a swashbuckling figure taking Perdita out of her banal future for a few minutes — that will last her forever. If we leave his provenance up for grabs he can believably vanish from the scene." He tilted his gaze to Stew, the cameraman. "You can add some fog in post-production, right? A dazzle for him to ride off into?"

Stew lifted his thumb in agreement. "The post-production crew will handle that."

"Right — ready for a run-through?" Humph swung his searchlight beam around them all.

"We haven't settled Court's costume yet!" Diamond objected.

Humph said, placidly, "I think His Horse Lordship might manage something for himself, right?"

Tansy nodded with enthusiasm.

Her husband, grinning, put an arm around her. "Don't get too excited, my beauty. Are you prepared to deal with D'Chevalier?"

I thought he was going full on D'Artagnan. Pip was disappointed. She rather fancied cavaliers. But maybe that was what Leopold meant. Chevalier . . . cavalier . . . they both had something to do with horses.

Tansy dropped her gaze demurely, then leaned into her husband while she rolled on the knee length stockings and slipped into the shoes. Amazingly, they fitted. Ward must have an incredible eye for sizing.

"Show on road," Humph said. His quiff bobbed as he rocked on his toes.

Pip waited for Magda to say something about proper procedure. Then she remembered Magda had always managed artists and their models until recently. She might not be too sure about normal filming procedure. But then — what did Pip know? She'd been out of the job herself for over a decade. Advances must have been made.

The Biblio-reps didn't seem troubled.

Humph must have thought they weren't reacting quickly enough, for he began moving like a sheepdog, gathering his flock and shooing them towards the entrance. Tansy, magnificent in the wedding dress, left the horse in her husband's charge, and walked ahead with Ward.

Pip watched several of the Biblio-reps surge out in the wake of the camera crew.

The men playing Oz, Stevo and the groomsman followed.

"Car," Pip heard one of them saying.

"Use my roadster," Humph replied. "Grand! It gets to cameo! It will forever be the iconic roadster from *Half-Life of the Lost.*"

"Shall I get it for you?" Matin Campania asked.

Pip turned to glance at him. She'd hardly noticed him among all the flamboyant characters.

Dialled down, she thought knowledgably. She was sure the vibrant Tamzin Campania would never be with a man as self-effacing as Matin seemed at this moment.

Humph nodded. "If you please . . .um . . ."

"Matin Campania."

"Yes. Do you know where it is?"

"I do."

Matin turned on his heel and reappeared very soon driving a scarlet vintage roadster in immaculate condition. He eased it towards the orchard, and Pip and Magda followed.

Somewhere ahead, a trumpet blared.

"What the hell was that?" Pip asked, hurrying to keep up with Magda's longer strides.

Magda sighed. "Search me. But young Leopold is a horse lord, so God alone knows what he's got up his sleeve."

CHAPTER EIGHT. THE SECOND BRIDE

They soon found out what Court Leopold was planning to wear in his role as the horseman.

On what Matin had called the greensward, the cameras were setting up.

Humph had taken possession of the roadster and donned a jaunty chauffeur's cap.

Pip and Magda parked themselves on hampers someone had brought along. Presumably, they contained costumes. Pip had to hitch herself up with an energetic bounce.

She accorded getting on and off too-tall seats as yet another accidental gift to her continuing fitness.

Magda said, "I could really use a Tom Cat Hill about now."

Pip thought she could use a drink too, and she fetched out her flask. She offered it to Magda, who sniffed it unenthusiastically and said she'd pass.

"It's camomile tea. I grew it in my garden."

"It's not the provenance . . . it's the stuff itself. Mum used camomile tea for calming the nerves. Never could take to the smell."

All the more for me.

Pip took a restorative sip.

"Mind if I join you?" Star Calder-Quince edged up beside Pip.

Pip shuffled over, noting the woman had no need to bounce. "You were in my dance rehearsal."

"Was that yours? I thought it was just a general dance-off." Star folded her hands in her lap. "I like to keep fit, and I'm going to need to for this shoot."

Pip frowned, wondering why. Then it occurred to her. "Oh, because you're going to be lying down for extended periods?"

"Pre-zackerly. It takes a lot of energy to lie down and pretend to be comatose." She gave a theatrical sigh. "And now Humph has come up with this plum scene—the origin scene for Perdita and the whole darned edifice—and I don't even get to feature in it. As my youngest would say—*Go figure.*"

"You could have done the stunt yourself," Pip said, remembering how she and Sully had carried the day when the director had tried to replace Tiny Pippin Pearmain with a stuntwoman during the abduction scene in *The House of Heriot*.

She recalled the awed expression on her young face as the camera zoomed in for a closeup. She had never been brave, but it was absolutely worth it.

Star said, "I like to believe I could have done it myself, but I know it really would have been an unacceptable risk, both for me and for the production. I suppose if I broke an ankle or something I could still be Perdita, but I'm going to ache quite enough from lying there as it is. Besides . . . Rox would be royally offended if I wilfully put myself in the way of structural damage."

Pip sighed. She had a fellow feeling for folk who weren't very brave. "Who's Rox? And is that rocks as in stones?"

"Rox as in Roxburghe. Him indoors. My husband." Star grinned and added, in obvious parentheses, "His grandmother named him. She was something of a grande dame. She even added an ultimate e to the end."

Pip reflected that she was hardly in a position to think anyone's name odd.

"Mind, it would be almost worth Rox's displeasure to be held in the arms of that pretty young man, on that very pretty horse . . ." Star mused.

"I got to do that once," Pip said.

"Really? You've been in a film with Court Leopold? Or do you mean something extra-curricular?"

"I mean in a general manner of speaking. And I'm not speaking about young Mister Leopold. This would have been before he was born. I was in a film called *The House of Heriot*. It would have been way before your time, too. My character got abducted by a highwayman. On a horse."

"It sounds thrilling," Star said in apparent amusement.

"It was."

"And did you make the most of the opportunity and seduce the highwayman?"

Pip thought about that. "I didn't. Anyway, I don't think it was ever an option. I was only sixteen."

"Oops," Star said.

"Not even my character did. I was playing younger than my age—fourteen, I think. The reviews had quite a bit to say regarding the chaste rapport that developed between the junior leads. There was one kiss—tres brotherly. Or do I mean cousinly . . . Here."

Pip tapped her forehead and took another sip of her tea.

"Is that green tea?" Star asked.

"Camomile," Magda said, surprising Pip, who had almost forgotten she was there. "An acquired taste."

"I drink parsley tea from time to time, but it's an affectation. I think I read somewhere that it's good for the kidneys. I actually prefer strong Indian tea with milk and sugar, which is not fashionable," Star said. She glanced up. "Aha. Showtime."

"Bit of hush!" someone yelled through a loudspeaker.

Everyone fell obediently silent.

"Prologue, take one," the same person said.

Pip felt her eyes bug as the horse appeared from the trees. She'd expected Leopold to be riding, but instead he was leading the beast. Both seemed transformed. Surely the horse had been smaller, and grey? Out in the sunshine it appeared more cream. Leopold had found a costume somewhere, full black cavalier pants tucked into polished boots, a voluminous shirt, a corsair hat with feathers, and a black cloak.

"Crumbs!" Star whispered, fanning herself. "That's enough to make me fanaticise about a bit of recreational bigamy!"

In one hand, he held a brass trumpet of the kind angels played in mediaeval paintings. Pip seemed to remember it was called a clarion.

Leopold led the horse through the scene, Diamond called *Cut,* and everyone relaxed.

Ward walked onto the set, ushering the bride.

The horse, seeing her, pranced excitedly.

Humph called, "That's what we want—can you do that again?"

"Assuredly, master," Leopold called, doffing his huge hat.

The horse plunged and he crammed the hat back on.

Tansy retreated a few steps, someone called *Action,* and the bride took the same few steps forwards, holding up her skirts. The horse pranced, the horseman bowed, scooped up the bride and arranged her on the horse. He leaped up behind her like a circus rider, tucked an arm around her waist, kissed her head through the veil and swung the horse around into a canter.

"Camera two. Pick up tracking shot."

"Camera three . . ."

"Cut!"

The scene went on, and Pip sat entranced, almost back in her exciting scene with Alain Barfleur on his wonderful horse, Varian.

She remembered it as being much smoother than this scene but then, of course, it had been properly scripted and blocked beforehand, and Alain had been an actor. Leopold was a singer and musician. They both rode beautiful horses, though, and from what she remembered and observed, they looked very similar.

But Alain was kind. Court Leopold is . . .

Pip tried to think of an appropriate adjective. Slick wasn't right. Charming, maybe. Languidly polished. That would do! But he seemed to love his wife, and if he was facile — there was a good one — then he'd surely have picked a she-dolly or runway model to marry rather than the earthy and straight-talking Tansy.

There was quite a long pause while Matin Campania, Jasper, Stew, and Humph held a confab and Ward tried to tidy the bride's skirts.

The horse took exception and danced about, snorting.

Star whispered, "Just look at that seat! She must have been riding forever!"

"Bit of hush! Now — roadster enters!"

There was a pause while Humph apparently remembered he was part of the scene and scurried over to his roadster. He bounced in, joining Oz, Stevo, and the groomsman, who must have scrambled into costume while the horse and rider were being filmed.

There was another long pause while the director organised cues for the horse to move into a gallop and the roadster to roar up hooting.

"Action!"

Pip didn't know where to look as four apparently inebriated men in formal attire tore up, whooping and yelling. At a nod from the director, Humph squeezed the old-fashioned bulb horn which honked raucously.

The galloping horse reared up on his haunches, raking his forehooves, the rider released the bride, and she slithered down, landing briefly on her feet before letting herself crumple into the grass.

The horse tore on.

The roadster swerved, and the men tumbled out and rushed to the fallen bride.

"Cut!"

The bride sat up, got to her feet and waved vigorously at the returning horse. Its rider leaped down and embraced the bride, who gave him a push. "Thou great gooby—thou dropped me on my arse!"

He laughed and objected that was what was supposed to happen.

Diamond shoved his fingers through his hair and looked unhappily over to Stew. "Did you get any of that?"

Stew stuck his thumb up. "Sure did. Some of it might even be usable."

Diamond blew his cheeks out. "From the top—"

Pip watched as the pieces of scene were run again, and this time she noticed one of the camera operators was filming the others . . . that must be for the making of documentary.

By now several other festival goers had crowded in to watch the scenes. Pip began to feel the need for some quiet, but escaping through the throng behind her seemed impossible.

After a long while, Diamond yelled, "Cut!" yet again.

There was some shuffling and a minor altercation between Ward and Tansy Leopold who, it devolved, did not want to relinquish the bride's dress.

It fell to Leopold to pacify her. He bent and whispered to her, and she turned her back so he could operate the zipper.

She emerged, somewhat crumpled, but apparently undamaged. A fair-haired woman came to speak with her and drew her out of the set, while Ward conversed with Leopold.

Pip couldn't hear what they said, but she gathered Leopold was to wait to film another piece of the scene.

"That'll be me," Star Calder-Quince remarked as Ward

beckoned her.

She headed off to change into the wedding dress.

Pip connected some mental dots. "They're going to film closeup inserts," she told Magda.

Magda said, "Is it always this disorganised?"

Pip considered. "Usually."

Star, as the bride, played through a brief insert of arriving at the photographic venue alone. She drifted along unhappily, saw the horse and rider, gazed at them with hope and desire, and accepted the rider's invitation. Leopold bent to scoop her into his arms.

"Cut!"

The second insert was shorter. Star lay down in the grass, and Ward arranged her like a doll, consulting his phone for the exact pose and fall of the dress and veil.

Leaving her crumpled in position he backed out of shot, the four men rushed forward and milled around the bride, trying to wake her, pulling her about.

Stew signalled that he had what he wanted, Diamond yelled *Cut,* and the men moved away.

Stew moved in for pick-up shots of the bride's face, dimly seen through the veil.

That, Pip supposed, was because Star Calder-Quince was too old for the twenty-something bride she was meant to be. The actors playing her husband and brother were also too old, but the focus would surely be on their costumes and drunken behaviour.

"Cut!" Diamond said for the last time.

There was more milling as everyone dispersed.

Pip was somewhat impressed. Despite the chaos, the unplanned scene seemed to have come off well. But still . . . it was just the one scene and it had taken quite long enough. How the devil were they going to fit the whole play into around ten days?

Chapter Nine. Break!

Pip was ready to return to cabin six for a while to enjoy some solitude, but the film crew had other ideas.

Diamond said, "We'll check on what we have in the can. I need Perdita, Nurse, Doctor, Stevo, Mother, Oz, and Solace on the hospital set. In costume, please."

That brought more milling until Ward said loudly, "I'll be Mother Duckie. Come along, darlings."

Pip realised with a jolt that she was about to start work.

The stage had been set up properly by now. There was a high hospital bed with machinery, a flickering monitor, and someone had laid in a sound track suggesting noise just outside the room.

Humph appeared stage left and fussed about, manhandling people into position. Pip, unscripted, backed into a corner near the door.

Star vanished briefly and returned dressed in a hospital gown, with her hair gathered into a kind of retro shower cap.

She hitched herself onto the high bed and sat with her feet dangling, reminding Pip momentarily of herself.

"Do I get a pillow? Am I lying flat?"

Humph bounced up and applied his hands to her shoulders. "Lie down, kiddo."

Star blew a raspberry at him but obeyed, swinging her legs around to lie flat. Someone cranked the bed to raise the head end a little, and three set dressers tried different sizes of pillow.

Someone brought a mass of tubing over. Humph shook his

head emphatically.

"But she's in a coma, dude—"

"Yes, but at this point she's classified as merely unconscious and expected to wake at any moment . . . second
thoughts, lose the shower cap."

The dresser shrugged and removed the tubing.

"Thanks, Humph," Star said. She pulled off the cap.

"Shush, you. You're in la-la-land in a coma."

Star stuck her tongue out. "I hope someone's bringing me
a coffee before I have to pass out. I positively cannot be comatose without caffeine."

Pip blinked. Just who was the director here?

Then she recalled this was a repertory society, and so might
have different behavioural expectations.

Humph was far more hands on with the asset than a playwright ought to be, especially these days.

She hoped nobody would sue him for manhandling an actor. Star didn't appear to mind, but sometimes *she didn't object
at the time* wasn't accounted a viable defence.

It would be utterly messy if someone sued Humph.

Matin Campania came in and said quietly that tea and coffee were available for the next twenty minutes.

A tall, fair man dressed in a shirt saying *Fee Kaffee* at *Arts in
Tune* took orders.

Pip asked, without much hope, for cambric tea, but he nodded, smiling, and asked if she'd like a cup or a mug. He
looked ever so slightly . . . something. Pip wondered if he was
another fairy.

The remaining actors, having learned their marks, moved
back, leaving Pip, Star, and Nurse in the room.

Tea and coffee was served along with small biscuits that
smelled of ginger and vanilla and with various rather ad-
vanced-looking slices.

Humph came and went.

Pip dusted powdered sugar off her fingers and moved to talk to Star. "How did you get cast as Perdita?"

Star, who was dangling her feet again and eating a piece of something heaped with blackberries and cream, said, deadpan, "Damned if I know. Maybe because I can lie still. Even if I go to sleep by mistake, I will be still. Rox occasionally used to prod me awake to see if I'd died and hadn't noticed. It's quite a talent, you know."

Pip did know. She ventured, "Would you have wanted to play Solace?"

"God, no! Humph was dead-determined to have Tiny Pippin Pearmain or no one. Solace is his pièce de resistance."

"But I was offered the screen test less than two weeks ago . . . When were you cast?"

Star said, "Humph got this deal going with *Diamond Spellman* and the *Arts in Tune* folk, and somehow sometime became next month at the festival, so there was a hustle on. The whole audition process was going to take too long, so Humph did what Humph does best . . ."

She paused, but Pip said nothing.

After a breath, Star continued, "He grabbed for the low-hanging fruit. I mean, he bowled up to one of our performances, nabbed me as I fell off the stage — " She caught herself up and laughed. "It was intentional, and I didn't pitch into the orchestra pit. I merely staggered into the wings with a flipping great prop dagger in my back. Anyhow, Humph ascertained I was dead-for-the-duration and dragged me out to a café he frequents. *Der Kaffeetanz*, it's called. Then he plied me with fancy cakes and sold me the idea of convincing the Bibs that our next project ought to be his phoenix of a play. He also informed me that I would be perfect as Perdita as I wouldn't have any lines to forget, and I can play dead nearly as well as his current dog. I think one of the kids trained it . . . anyone's for a biscuit, that dog.

"I nearly crowned him—Humph that is—with a slab of buttered stollen for that jab. Then he launched into his spiel about Solace having to be played by Tiny Pippin Pearmain. The man was like a broken record. He kept waving a picture of you at me to make his point." She bit into the blackberry contraption and cackled.

"What picture?" Pip asked, diverted.

"You were holding giant feather fans and looking glassy-eyed. You'd actually let go of one fan and there was just the merest nip-slip on view."

"That would be from a play called *Swan*," Pip said. "I played a fan dancer. I didn't know there was a photo of it. Better get one for my show reel."

"Good luck wresting that away from Humph. It's one of his treasures. And not, I assure you, because of the nip-slip. He's not that sort of man." She cackled again. "God, you should have heard him ranting when nobody could find you! Where were you hiding, by the way—and why? Surely you weren't scared of being Humphed? He's hutterly armless . . . if you know what I mean."

Pip felt somewhat swept away by this flood of talk, but she sensed no malice in Star, so she said, cautiously, "My agent at *Sullivan Gilbert* went to glory . . . I mean, she—"

"I get it," Star said, looking sympathetic. "That's why one needs young agents—but not too young, if you know what I mean. The too-youngs either overestimate one's prowess or underestimate one's experience."

Pip went on, "It was back in two thousand and twelve. I stayed on the agency books, but I just never really heard from them again. It didn't help that I moved."

"Oh, one of those situations." Star nodded. "One of Humph's sons is an author, and he wrote eight books for *Kittenclaw Press*. The company was taken over, then sold again, and when Ceddie got in touch with them about a new series idea, they told him politely that they dealt only with authors already on their books. As my kids would say, Go figure."

That wasn't quite the situation, since she hadn't left a forwarding address, but Pip nodded anyway. "What happened?"

"Ceddie informed them of their error and listed his titles with them, chapter, verse, publication dates, and sales figures. Their response was, Oh, okay . . . As he said they could hardly have been less interested, so, being a fairly confident young man, he offered the series to another company." She grinned. "It hit the big time!"

"What did they say? The original company?"

Star shrugged. "I doubt if they ever knew. Ceddie went dark on them . . . and he bound the new company to secrecy regarding his real name. Big mystery. He put clues in the new books, but evidently, no one has ever discovered the answer, so the prize for guessing the author's identity remains unclaimed."

"You know, though."

"Oh, I know. And wild horses . . . et cetera."

Pip was good at keeping secrets, so she respected that.

"We were all glad when Humph said you'd been dug up from under your rock," Star went on. "He was threatening to pull the plug if you weren't found, pronto."

Pip wanted to say playwrights didn't have that much power, but she'd already noted nothing about this production seemed normal to her, so she held her fire. Something occurred to her then, and she narrowed her eyes at Star.

"What?"

The woman crossed her arms.

"Humph didn't know you when he came in earlier. He asked who you were."

"Oh." Star's face creased up. "Oh, that. Yes, Humph does that."

"Why?"

"He has prosopagnosia — face blindness. He's pretty good at compensating, and I should think he'll know you."

"He didn't seem to recognise me when he recorded the music," Pip recalled.

"He probably didn't associate you with dancers, and he wouldn't had had his aide memoire — cue the nip-slip-pic — in his hand. But still, even if you change your clothes he can maybe pick you by your size when you're on-set or somewhere he expects you to be."

Pip almost said he wasn't all that big himself, but at that point the smiling blond serving man came round to collect cups, and Ward and three female assistants converged with powder puffs and pancake and wet-wipes to de-sticky the performers.

Ward pounced on Pip, demanded to know why she wasn't in costume, and marched her off to convene with a pair of overalls and a grey shirt while the scripted cast made their first run-through.

"Hat?" she asked hopefully, but Humph popped up and said she'd have to wait. "In the first scene you're waking up and discovering yourself . . . hence the grey shirt."

Pip looked down at her green daisy-toed shoes which she was wearing for luck, then away again, in case someone made her take them off. Humph and Ward were just as likely to shove her into cowboy boots . . .

She was allowed to watch the second run-through and take note of the infinitesimal pauses that marked her cues for input. She made mental notes, blocked her movements in the third go-round and dropped her lines into the scene in the fourth.

"Cut!"

Pip jumped. She'd folded as Solace reached the height of bewilderment that no one reacted to her presence.

After the screen test at *Diamond Spellman Studio*, when Jasper Diamond and Matin read lines for her, she'd wondered what the other actors would do while she spoke and moved. Now she discovered it varied. Sometimes they continued their moves and mimed lines, and at other times they went into freeze-frame. She'd been thinking of them as a haphazard amateur rep, but she realised they were both flexible and experienced.

"Break!"

She jumped again as a burst of applause broke from various un-used cast who'd been watching in silence from behind the cameras.

Humph was beaming like a dog with a stolen roast chicken.

Or maybe a bantam rooster in possession of a cornfield. Pip felt giddy with exhaustion.

CHAPTER TEN. THE PORTRAIT

With that first scene in the can, Pip and most of the others were released for a two-hour break.

Star and Nurse remained, and three bridesmaids came onstage to do the first walk-through of a later scene in which they prepared for another wedding and uncomfortably reminisced about their comatose friend.

Pip glanced at Magda. "Ought I to stay?"

Magda said, "You were released, so if I were you, I'd scarper. Just be back for the next call."

"That's for lunch," Stew the cameraman said, having overheard them in a sudden lull. "The *Fee Kaffee* people are organising it al fresco. The real next call will be at two."

Magda said, "Thank you!" She added to Pip, "Let me know if they ask anything of you that they shouldn't. I seriously need to brush up on industry standards."

Pip said she would. She left the sound stage and walked out into the festival.

There were a great many things she wanted to see and do, but she also desired quiet, so she headed back towards cabin six.

Halfway there, she remembered Magda would be returning there soon. She'd agreed to room with her agent, but too much togetherness wasn't her style.

Instead, she veered off in the direction of an airy wooden building she thought was the barn. Matin had said it contained a pony and a horse, and probably goats, but she was prepared to spend time with those. The goats were intelligent,

so they'd give up on her when they discovered she was gin-
gerbread-free.

*There might be a hayloft where I can look out the window and see
the festival spread out before me.*

She found the double doors of the barn propped open and
peered inside. She expected it to be dim and dusty, maybe
with motes of hay floating in barred sunshine filtering in
through cracks. To her perplexity, the barn was lit up with a
lovely golden glow.

She looked up automatically, almost expecting a chande-
lier, but instead she saw a wide skylight with storm-shutters
on either side. There was a hayloft, but it was on a mezzanine
level, forming a kind of gallery to allow the skylight to cast its
radiance uninterrupted.

"Wow!" The floor was scattered with straw, and bales and
bundles of hay formed an interesting terrain. It appeared to
be untenanted, unless she counted a twitter of sparrows
perched high in the rafters.

The goat ballet sprang into mind. Maybe haybales were in-
appropriate, but knolls and hummocks would absolutely be
the way to go.

Pip wished Master Capricorn, the herdfee piper, would
wander in so she could get him to play the goat music for her.
What had Jane called it?

Chorós Capricornus.

She listened to the music again in her mind's ear and began
sketching steps.

*All these years and you've spent them pottering about the cottage
and garden,* she berated herself. *Now you're actually busy and
you start creating imaginary ballets! Are you nuts?*

She concluded she probably was, but it was hardly a new
thought, so she set it aside.

She was well away with two piping goatherds competing
to lure one another's goats when she heard something rustle
behind her.

Pip, to whom rustling generally meant Kittisack was doing something he shouldn't, spun round in an accidental pirouette.

Someone was perched on a haybale, holding a large open sketchbook and a stick of charcoal.

After a startled moment, Pip recognised the violinist who had led the supergroup for Dancing in the Dawn.

Tamzin Campania.

She looked less startled than Pip felt, but then, she had every right to be sketching in the barn. It was her barn.

Pip felt unaccustomedly foolish.

"I hope I didn't disturb you."

Tamzin tossed back her wavy brown hair and smiled. "Not at all," she said pleasantly.

"But I expect you came here for a bit of quiet?"

"I did ... My old nanny is watching Music and the dogs for a while. Not an imposition, truly. She's not an actual nanny anymore, but she loves the little ones, as she calls them. The difficulty is not to get her to be with them, but to get her to leave when it's time. We usually have to arrange another get-together—soon—to ease the transition."

"What music? Is someone playing?"

As soon as the words were out, Pip knew that was a silly question to ask at a dance festival.

Tamzin may have thought so too, but she said, "I'm sure someone is. Lots of someones are playing all over the place, but in this case I was referring to our daughter. Music Alexandra Delphinium Campania."

"What a glorious name!"

"We think so." Tamzin paused, then added, "Music because it means so much to both of us, Alexandra because it's a kind of family name . . ."

"Delphinium for the flower or the island?"

"Both, partly, but it has another meaning. See?"

Tamzin lifted a braided cord she wore around her neck, bringing the pendant into view. It was a wooden dolphin. "Delphinium—"

"Is sort of Greek for dolphin," Pip broke in. She added, "I saw some dolphins, and now I'm making a ballet called *Delphine.*"

"I know," Tamzin said calmly.

"How?"

"You were dancing part of it earlier, along with some of the *Forevers*, a stray *Dad Ballet* man, and one of the actors from the film. You're in the film too, right?"

"How did you know?"

Tamzin indicated the dress Pip had changed back into. "Film Star."

"Oh—that. I'm not a star, but yes, I'm playing a character named Solace."

Tamzin said, "I don't know much about the film. Matin— my husband—is involved with it, but I'm tied up with the music and painting side of things. I came in here between sessions to catch up on a few things, but seeing you got me sidetracked." Her eyes crinkled in a mischievous smile. "Want to see?"

See what? But Tamzin evidently wanted to share, so Pip moved over and perched on the next bale.

Tamzin passed her the sketchbook.

Pip looked down at—herself. "Goodness!" She gazed at the picture in dawning delight. The artist hadn't flattered her. She was poised on tiptoe with her arms raised, but she lacked the smooth lines of the younger dancers she'd seen that morning. Her elbows interrupted the perfect balletic curve she'd never been able to achieve, and her hair was ruffled and sliding out of its bun. What pleased her was the arch of her feet and the joyful expression on her face.

"That's me. That's exactly the way I feel when I'm dancing!" Tears prickled her eyes, and she felt a most uncharacteristic desire to hug the young woman before her.

"I'm glad you approve," Tamzin said.

"But how did you know?"

"I saw it. Besides, that's the way I feel when I'm playing my fiddle."

Pip blinked, seeing rainbows through her wet eyelashes.

Tamzin watched her sympathetically as she reached out to reclaim her sketchbook.

Pip supposed she must be used to such reactions. As when Zennor St Ives had guessed she'd been reading the Orders of the Fay series, she felt annoyed at being predictable.

Tamzin said, "I've always felt so lucky to have things in my life that make me joyful. I had a most peculiar childhood, but I almost always had something wondrous in compensation. Of course, the downside is if you lose it."

Pip put a few things together in her mind. "Matin said something about your foster brothers. Those would be the two pisky muties?"

"Yes."

If Tamzin was startled at hearing Pip using the term, she didn't betray her feelings. But then, she was married to an elf, so Pip was sure she knew all about such things.

"I take it you've met them?"

"One of them gave your husband some grief at the boom-gate yesterday."

"That'd be Mull, I suppose. He's marginally more annoying than Zen, and he loves winding Matin up."

"And I saw them both—and some of their family—at the Fairy Gardens in Sydney recently."

That seemed to surprise her companion. "What were they doing there?"

Pip explained about the construction work at the dog park which had led the Dames with Dogs club to move temporarily to another venue.

"Oh, I see. I'm a Dame myself — their club artist — but I haven't been to the get-togethers recently on account of Music getting mobile and preparing for the festival. I also have a new riding pony — well, a horse, really — so every chink of my time . . . What's the matter?"

"Nothing. Just I met some of the Dames with Dogs and one of them mentioned you — only I didn't know it was you. She just talked about their club artist. Caddy, her name was. She had a white dog called Mary-Mary."

Tamzin nodded. "I expect she told you I'd want to paint you if I'd been there. So I would."

"You drew me already." Pip indicated the sketch.

"Yes, but that's for the festival scrapbook. I'm catching as many interesting people as I can. Caddy's right though — I really would like to paint you, a bit more formally. Would you mind?"

"No, and come to think of it, your husband suggested it too. It might be difficult to fit in with everything else, though." She brightened. "I suppose you could do it from a photo."

"That would be the most practical solution, but I always paint from life, or occasionally from memory. It wouldn't take long. It wouldn't be huge. Mind you, the court portraits I sometimes do take much longer than you'd think. They're small enough to fit on a coin or a seashell and they take a lot of focus, magnification, and the finest brushes you ever saw." She drew her brows together. "Would you like to keep that sketch?"

"I'd love to," Pip said promptly. "But you said you needed it for the scrapbook."

"I do, but that's electronic. I can scan it in and give you the original, then paint you. Deal?"

"Deal!" Pip remembered she wanted to ask about music and copyright for *Delphine,* but Tamzin suddenly tore the sketch out of the book.

"No, I'll give you this one now. I can easily do another sketch for the collection, and besides, this one wasn't quite cricket. You probably thought you were enjoying yourself in private."

Pip was aware the sketch had just become exponentially more precious to her as a unique piece. She was trying to formulate an appropriate *thankyou* and work up to a question as to whether Tamzin ever did decoupage when she saw the page the sketch had previously covered.

CHAPTER ELEVEN. REUNION

Pip stared at the coloured picture on the page. It wasn't finished, but there was enough of it to make her certain of what she saw.

"Wh—" Her mouth went dry and she licked her lips and tried again. "Are those your cats?"

Tamzin contemplated the drawing. "We don't have cats at the moment. Dogs, goats, ponies, a baby . . . but not cats. I like cats, and so does Matin, but they just haven't happened for us yet." She looked up. "Cats do tend to happen, apparently. A friend of mine always had cats happening—coming and going, and visiting at his place . . . Why do you ask?"

Pip looked at the picture again. It showed three cats—one backlit by the sun, another picked out in more detail, and a shadowy third. The first was a Siamese with an assertive nose. The second was a smaller animal coloured in a smudgy pattern of gold, brown, toffee and white. The last one was part of a floral pattern.

Kittisack and Amberjill—and maybe Lupin's cat.

It wasn't them. It must be a chance resemblance, because they presented as a Siamese tom, a calico queen, and a pottery guardian. It wasn't them, but it *was* an inexact reproduction of a page from *Grandmother's Sunshine*.

"May I look?" Her lips felt cold and stiff.

Tamzin seemed puzzled, but she handed the book back.

Pip examined the picture with exquisite care. It wasn't a perfect copy of the illustration she knew. Some details were wrong. The calico cat had its tail curved instead of straight.

The gently blowing curtain that formed a natural side frame had single gold leaves instead of twigs and bunches. The shadowy third cat was wreathed in flowers of just the wrong shade of pinkish blue.

The slight differences in detail reminded Pip of the various versions of mediaeval paintings, sometimes done by the original artist as test pieces or revisions, and sometimes credited to the school of . . .

"What's up? You look as if you've seen a ghost." Tamzin sounded concerned.

"I have — sort of. You paint from life. Where did you see these cats?"

Tamzin picked up a stick of what looked like coloured wax or crayon and used the sharpened edge to add a new petal to the third cat's garland.

Pip waited. She had no impression that the artist was prevaricating. It was more as if she was choosing how to express her answer.

After several seconds that felt like minutes, Tamzin looked up, frowning in thought. "I know what I said, and it's true, but I also said I occasionally draw from memory. I did a lot of that a few years ago when I spent time alone on an island. I started drawing people I'd known to keep from going nuts with loneliness." She raised one hand and dropped it again, allowing the light to catch on a glittering bracelet. Pip saw the clasp was carved in the form of two wooden dolphins.

Tamzin said, "These aren't real cats — at least, I don't think so. They come from a book I loved a long time ago when I was small. It was a dear little book. I loved it because it was magical and . . . and joyful."

"Do you still have it?" Pip asked, trying to sound no more than gently curious.

"It was never mine. It belonged to a lady who taught me dancing. I'm glad it wasn't mine, because my parents didn't believe in keeping things for more than two or three years. The only thing I have from my childhood is a little dancing tunic, and I don't quite know how that survived the regular culls. I'm keeping it for Music when she's big enough to wear it. Won't be long, at the rate she's growing."

"That's all you have?" Pippin, a lifelong hoarder, wasn't sure whether to be envious or appalled.

"That's all—but although they could take the things away, and refuse to let me talk about them, they couldn't take my memories. I'm recreating whatever I can from those years to show to Music when she's old enough to ask how she came to be. It's Project Music."

Pip hugged herself as a shiver ran down her spine. She deliberately poked the bear. "Wouldn't it be easier to get a copy of the book so it would be exactly as you remember?"

"That was my first idea when I first decided on Project Music. She's too young to follow stories yet, but she likes pictures and rhymes. I asked about the book in a few shops in Sydney, including antiquarians, but none of them had a copy. I looked online, but no luck there either. I found occasional references to it in readers' forums, but always from people like me, trying to find a copy. Then I did what I ought to have done in the first place—called a shop that specialises in rare titles and local authors—they keep copies of every volume in a series and that's quite unusual. My old friend Emily writes for children, and all her books are there. So is a series she and I both loved when we were young."

"An old friend?"

Tamzin smiled. "Are you trying to catch me out in a fib? It's not one, you know. We were best-friends-forever when we were nine or ten and living in Adelaide. After my family moved on to Darwin—and no, I wasn't told we were going until we'd left—I wasn't allowed to contact her but . . . quite recently I did. She remembered me, though not by the name I have now, of course. We're friends-forever again, and we're working on a lovely new project."

Pip said, "Would that shop you mentioned be *The Orange Grove?*"

"It is! You know it, then?"

"I'm a member of their Frequent Reader program—at the super-pager level."

"Wow! A super-pager!" Tamzin sounded properly impressed, but also a wee bit mocking. Pip was reminded of Zennor St Ives' playacting when his mother told him about Pip's role in *The House of Heriot*.

Pip said sheepishly, "I'm a bit—compulsive."

"Oh, I quite understand. So am I. Creative people often are."

"I take it you didn't get a copy of the book, though?" Pip asked.

Tamzin smudged the pink-blue colour of the petal with her thumb, blooming it into lupin-blue, frowned, and picked up a stick in a different tint. "That needs to be more apricot." Then she added, regretfully, "No. It's the first time I've ever stumped Jonquil Orange on a title. Usually when I ask for things, she says either that they have it or that they can get it or, occasionally, that she'll keep her ear to the ground. Well, you'd know that, right?" She looked up and Pip nodded.

"But this time she told me flat out that she not only couldn't get a copy but that the book probably didn't exist, and had never existed, at least, not under the title I remember. I'm sure it did, though. The pictures I remember had to come from somewhere. Jonquil believes I must be recalling one of the mid-twentieth-century *Sunshine* series that came out annually between nineteen thirty and nineteen sixty-five. I've tracked down three of those. They all have a series look about them, and although they sound the same from a verbal or written description—collections of illustrated stories and verse— they're utterly different from what I remember. For one thing, the later ones have strong block colours and sharp-edged drawings—very mid-century American. As you can see from this copy, the book I remember used soft watercolours and smudgy outlines. Magical is the best adjective, although even that isn't quite it."

"Do you remember any other pictures from the book well enough to reproduce them?" Pip asked.

"There was one of dancing goats, and another one of a white pony with a leprechaun man. I think that story was called *The Gifted One*. It was about a pony that never grew old—maybe. There was one picture of a waterfall, and one of a black puppy, and lots of others."

Pip realised she was nodding in agreement. She knew, of course, exactly what book Tamzin Campania was remembering, and she nearly had her ducks in a row.

What she couldn't understand was how someone else's childhood memories tied in with her own experiences.

She had taught children to dance at the Apples and Pears playgroup back in Delmsford in the 1990s. She had shared a precious book with a child who loved music, dancing, and drawing.

That child had not been called Tamzin, but the mother had insisted that her daughter should have only new things.

The family had disappeared without warning, and her recent attempts to trace them online had failed.

The little girl had been around five, and the family might have gone to Adelaide.

It had to be true. Coincidence had a long arm, but not even Tiny Pippin Pearmain could believe in a coincidental arm as long as this.

She contemplated Tamzin Campania, trying to see in her the child she had known twenty-five years before. Her hair was still wavy, but darker. Her voice was different, but then, it would be.

She considered hinting and trailing possibilities, but her efforts to mislead Jonquil and Magda and even Cousin Jan about her heirloom book had left her feeling vaguely grubby.

She said, abruptly, "I haven't introduced myself to you, have I."

Tamzin said, "No. I probably should know who you are, since you're an actor, but I spent a great deal of the last decade off the grid. You look a bit familiar, so perhaps I have seen pictures of you somewhere?"

"You being off the grid wouldn't have made any difference, because Solace is my first part in eleven years," Pip said dryly. "Even before that I wasn't what you'd call a household name. I was in odd little plays, and in indie films before that term was invented, and television serials shown once and only rarely repeated."

"Are you absolving me for not knowing your name, then?"

"I'd have been astonished if you had known it. You're the wrong demographic, for one thing. My name's Pippin Pearmain—and yes, that is two types of apples."

"Is it a stage name?" Tamzin asked.

"No, it's the one my parents gave me. Pippin Picotee Pearmain, if you want the whole thing." She recalled how Tamzin had detailed her daughter's name and followed suit. "Pippin because Mum's family liked names from the garden and orchard, and because it went with Little Dad's name, Picotee because it was my paternal grandmother's name . . . and is also sort of a flower name . . . and Pearmain because that was the surname Little Dad happened to have."

"Pippin Picotee Pearmain. I love it! How lucky you are to have had just one name, and such a splendid one," Tamzin said warmly. She added, "I've had far too many of them." She smiled directly at Pip. "But then, you knew me by one of them, once upon a time—right?"

"I thought so, but I couldn't be sure." Pip sighed and

explained. "I think — I'm sure — I knew you a long time ago when you were four or five. You were called Angie Blake. Angela, probably, but your mother called you Angie. Angie-pangie sometimes."

Tamzin grimaced. "Angie Blake certainly was one of my names — it's the earliest one I remember, actually."

"And you liked Butterfly Princess things, and dancing and stories, and drawing. I used to mind you when your mum went to the shops, and we all went to the playgroup on Fridays, if I wasn't working."

Tamzin put down her drawing things. "You must be the little dancing lady I sometimes remember. You gave me a kaleidoscope, and you were the one who had the book — *Grandmother's Sunshine*." She stared at Pip. "I should have known you, but it was so long ago, and I thought you might be a dream. You're not my granny, are you? It would be lovely if you were."

Pip shook her head regretfully.

"No, of course not. You're not old enough." Tamzin sighed. "I think most people remember things from childhood because their family talk about them, and so the memories reinforce. My parents never wanted to talk about anything but now, so my memories never had the chance to reinforce."

Pip said, "Not long ago, I made a few half-hearted efforts to contact you, or your parents. I hoped you might have grown up to do something in the arts. I thought you might be a dancer or a dancing teacher."

"I love dancing, but I don't do it professionally. Why did you want to find me after all this time?"

"It was always a long shot, and it sounds silly and trivial now, but I had a lovely and very special holiday and after that, I started inventing a ballet — *Delphine* — "

Tamzin nodded comprehension.

"And I thought it would be nice to stage it instead of just having it on paper. I was going to ask the school where I live if I could work with some of their children, but I don't have teaching qualifications. I remembered dancing with the children in Delmsford, and with you, especially. I hoped you might give me a reference . . ." She shrugged. "Saying that out loud makes me realise how daft an idea it was, and what an imposition it would have been to expect you to remember me. I'd have been better off going back to the play group, although probably there's no one left who'd know I ever lived there. The children would be your age by now, and the teachers have probably retired or been transferred. The group might not exist anymore."

"I would have been happy to recommend you, but I doubt if it would carry any weight. I'm a portraitist and musician, not a dancer."

"No need now. The dance troupe—the *Forevers*—are going to work on it with me. And by the way, I was planning to talk to you about suitable music in the public domain."

Tamzin laughed. "I'm sure we can come up with something. I know a lot of music that's never been restricted, and a lot that can be adapted. I'm playing for some of the dance workshops anyway, so if you come along to those, we can all work together."

"That sounds perfect," Pip said, adding silently *As long as I can fit it in around the filming.*

She had yet another idea, this time about *Grandmother's Sunshine,* but that one she kept to herself. Before she could air it to anyone, she had to talk to Clarkia.

She was about to return to cabin six or go to lunch—she was unsure which because she'd lost track of time—when Tamzin said, "Tell me some of the other names in your family."

Pip said, "Little Mum's name was Rose. You might just remember her from when you came to visit us?"

"Sorry." Tamzin shook her head.

"Okay. Little Dad was Jonathan."

"Another apple!"

"Yes! My aunt was Helen. That's not a flower, but her actual name was Hellebore . . . the winter rose. Nanna Laurel's first name was Schizanthus. Nanna Pearmain—"

Tamzin lifted her finger. "Picotee—right?"

"Yes. My cousins were Juniper and Lupin, and Juniper's daughter is Clarkia."

"A proper garden of names," Tamzin said. "How far back does the floral theme go?"

"I don't know. One of our ancestors was called Aster, and she had grandchildren whose names were Cammie and Callie. We think they might really have been Camellia and Callistemon or something like that, but it's no more than a guess. And that's all I know."

Tamzin said, "It's a great deal more than I know. It took me years to extract my original name and my parents' real names from them, and even now they won't tell me anything more. I might see what I can find out from other routes one day—when I have time—or maybe I can get Matin to have a go at them."

"So they weren't called Alison and Chad Blake?" Pip asked, having dredged the names back to the forefront of her mind.

"No. Their birth names were Adelie Jane Spenser and Paul Bysshe-Minister and apparently their families didn't get along."

"Capulet and Montague?"

"Something like that, but they didn't die in a crypt. I was originally named Alexandra. I can't remember ever using it, though."

"You still gave it to your baby."

Tamzin shrugged. "It's a family name of a sort. I have so

115

little left from back then, and it is a lovely name. Fortunately Matin's family is the very opposite of mine. Lirrin—that's his mum, who is as lovely as her name—is working up a family tree for her grandchildren, so Music will know her dad's side of the family, at least." She frowned. "What I told you about my parents' names is what they told me, and only after a lot of pressing when Matin and I trapped them in a café. It might not be true. To be honest, I don't think I'd believe my father if he told me shoes came in pairs. My mother is slightly less mendacious. Maybe. And she did send me the tunic for Music. I see her occasionally, though not by arrangement. Make no mistake, she and my father are joined at the hip, but I like to think maybe she was just following along." She paused and added, half reluctantly, "They're not wicked, or even cruel. They treated me well enough and even loved me, within the confines of their—lifestyle."

Pip hummed briefly. She'd never known Chad Blake except by sight, but she did remember Alison, who had undoubtedly loved little Angie.

"With a surname like your father's, it should be possible to find out something," she said, remembering Magda's suggestion that Little Nanna Laurel's first name was a gift to the hopeful genealogist.

"It should be, but I've never seen it recorded anywhere. As I said, I'm not a bit sure he told me the truth about that—or anything. The whole Montague and Capulet thing could be an invention—an excuse to behave in a way unbefitting to a son-in-law. I would like to know something about my grandparents one day, if only for Music's sake." She got up and stretched, dismissing the subject. "Miss . . . Missus . . . um?"

"Just Pip will be fine. That's what you used to call me."

"Pip, then. I have to go and feed Music before the next sessions, but I do want to work with you on the ballet music, and I really want to do your portrait. Can we make a time now, or —"

Pip said, "I'll get a schedule from the director if I can, but if not before, I'll be dancing in the dawn with you tomorrow."

"Then I'll see you there," Tamzin said.

Pip remembered her ballet practice which she did a seven o'clock every morning, and her immovable date with hot water and lemon at eight.

Then she looked at her beautiful sketch of dancing for joy and cast her routine to the island winds. Some things were more important than self-imposed routines.

"I'll see you then," she agreed. "By the way, do you know how to do decoupage?"

Tamzin stared at her.

"Um. No. Do you?"

"Not yet," Pip said, and she left the airy sunlit barn and walked out into the magical festival.

ABOUT THE AUTHOR

Lark Westerly loves writing series where characters weave in and out of one another's stories.

She also loves playing with ideas and notions and researching odd information.

Lark lives in the island state of Tasmania, where she walks dogs, invents recipes, and rapidly reduces her garments to things the category of *shabby not-chic*. She rarely wears a matching pair of socks.

Unlike Pippin Pearmain, Lark is not tiny, not an only child, not single and not an on-screen performer. She knows quite a bit about her ancestry. She never learned ballet and she can't speak Cat-Morse. She has never tried decoupage, as most crafts are definitely above her paygrade. She doesn't even have a bucket list. Nevertheless, Pippin Pearmain and Lark Westerly are sisters under the skin.

Oh . . . you were wondering about that bucket that inspired *Performing Pippin Pearmain*? It happened like this . . .

To find out, visit

https://performingpippinpearmain.weebly.com/about-the-bucket.html